MW01026906

THE
ROBERT OLEN BUTLER
PRIZE STORIES
2005

THE
ROBERT OLEN BUTLER
PRIZE STORIES
2005

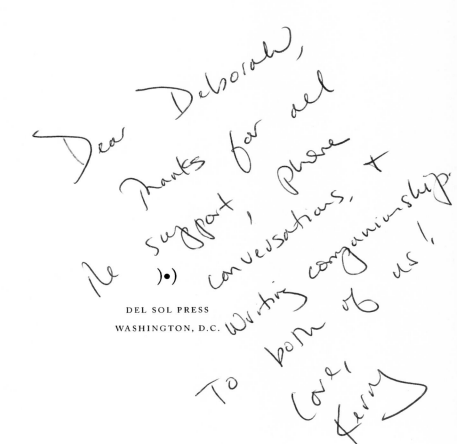

)•)

DEL SOL PRESS
WASHINGTON, D.C.

Dear Deborah,
Thanks for all
the support, phone
conversations, +
Writing companionship.
To both of us!,
Love,
Kerry

The Robert Olen Butler Prize Stories 2005

Copyright © 2006 by Del Sol Press. All rights reserved.

DEL SOL PRESS, WASHINGTON, D.C.

Paper ISBN: 0-9748229-8-1

FIRST EDITION

COVER PHOTOGRAPH BY MICHAEL BARAN

COVER DESIGN BY ANDER MONSON

INTERIOR DESIGN BY JASON REDERSTORF

Publication by Del Sol Press/Web del Sol Association, a not-for-profit corporation under section 501 (c) (3) of the United States Internal Revenue Code.

❧ Contents ❧

❧ *Acknowledgments* ❧

Thanks to the following magazines, in which the following stories originally appeared.

Jacob M. Appel, "Shell Game with Organs," *Boston Review*
Alicia Gifford, "Gorgeous World," *Confrontation*
Alison Lee Kinney, "Term," *The Literary Review*
Phil LaMarche, "In the Tradition of My Family," *Ninth Letter*
Jeff Parker, "The Taste of Penny," *Ploughshares*
Matthew J. Sullivan, "Unfound," *The Florida Review*
Alia Yunis, "A Nearly Blonde Christmas," *MIZNA*

The 2005 Prize Winner

❧ *Unfound* ❧

MATTHEW J. SULLIVAN

"Before the light, there was only darkness."
      —*opening lines of the Maori creation story*

"You're only as sick as your secrets."
      —*Denis Johnson, Resuscitation of a Hanged Man*

Chris, my best friend, is dying of a gunshot wound to the face in Oakland General Hospital. I should be down there assisting him in his last moments of life, but instead I'm cutting through the clouds, strapped inside an airplane that's headed for New Zealand.

A few hours ago, Oakland passed below. I watched it through the plane's scratched window—legos in a sandbox, bridges made of matchsticks—and imagined that I could see the floral lawn and helipad of the hospital. Then it was gone, and far below my feet a dark sheet of water reflected ripples of regret.

What happened to Chris was this: two days ago, he took his fiancée, a hippie nurse named Lori, out for a picnic in the grassy underarm of the Bay Bridge. As he spread out a lunch of chicken and champagne, she waited in the car, tapping her fingers in anticipation. Glowing romantic, Chris danced back to get her, and some Junkypunk out of nowhere cracked a pistol against his front teeth, said something cinematic no doubt—*Handover the cash or you're a fuggin' ghost*—and Chris, a real knuckle-cracker full of laughs with a spine like a railroad tie, simply spat on the grass.

Goodnight, Chris: Junkypunk ran away with the picnic.

Lori called me from the hospital. She told me about the shooting, but for the coldness of her voice she may as well have been announcing an offer for cheap long distance. She certainly didn't say anything about my last trip to Oakland, when she and I had somehow bumped into kitchen-table sex as Chris shaved in the shower. We'd been making breakfast in our bathrobes and the impulsive way it happened baffled us both—in a simple moment of spilled orange juice and cinnamon toast, we exploded our bond to a world beyond Chris. There was little comfort in the fact that our mistake immediately dragged us out of the breakfast nook and into regret. I'm convinced Chris never had a suspicion, but I've always wondered if Lori let our secret slide.

On the phone, instead of asking her, I listened. She informed me that Chris, if his brain weren't buried in gauze and drenched in Demerol, would want me there to escort him toward the alleys of death. She spoke, I envisioned: holding his hand as he yowled in the dark, guiding him around the falling water and garbage cans, telling the shadowman beneath the blanket how my life would lose a scoop when his final breath whisped through a tube.

When Lori offered to wire me money for the plane ticket to Oakland and mentioned how expensive these last-minute flights are, I was tempted to tell her to count me out and double-up the Demerol. I was tempted to tell her to haul a turntable into the ICU and spin Johnny Cash's version of "Long Black Veil" until Chris eased away. He'd want that ballad of betrayal more than my callused hand—we're old friends, I know deep things about him—but this was no longer about Chris. This was already about those of us alive.

I told her to wire me the money. I told her to pick me up at

Oakland's airport.

Estimated Time of Arrival in New Zealand: 11 hours, 47 minutes.

Things haven't been going well lately. Something's wrong with everyone.

The last trip I took—a credit card excursion to Vietnam in search of my father's remains—unfound—stranded me in a funk of disappointment. I expected that the journey would move me in deep and magnificent ways, but as the weeks clipped past, my sense of self remained as absent as my father's bones.

As soon as I'd arrived back in Denver, I took a cab to my girlfriend's apartment, expecting to find flowers and wine and warmth. Instead, I saw that the intimate postcards I'd mailed from Hanoi were face down on her rain-soaked porch. My key no longer worked, and a creepy stranger told me through the mailslot that she'd packed up and fled for Chicago weeks before—not a word to me.

Maybe worst of all was that when I made it to my apartment, eager to sulk in my sunken bed, I was scraped by one of those sights that will never leave my mind. I'd had an old friend sublet the place while I was gone, and when I opened the door, I caught a peripheral glimpse of him running naked from my bed to the bathroom with my bread knife dangling out of his ass, its handle disappeared. Everything was a tumble of ashtrays and uzo bottles. A blow-up doll caked with Cool-Whip yawned on my couch, silently shouting "Welcome Home!"

I set down my backpack and left for a walk, thinking my friend might clean up and forget his panic and shame. When I returned later, my backpack was stolen, my boxspring was broken, and my friend was gone. I found my kitchen knife sitting on the back of the toilet, covered in lotion and blood. A friend shouldn't do that to a friend, unless there's something wrong, and like I said, with everyone, there is these days.

—

My true intent was to visit Chris at the hospital in Oakland, but on the way out the door to catch the airport bus I stopped by my mailbox. Inside I found bills, some mail-ordered Air Supply cds, and an envelope holding a gaggle of kiwi stamps in its corner.

I'd never seen a stamp from New Zealand because Daryl, the only friend I have who lives down there, isn't the letter-writing sort. Daryl's not the anything-sort, actually, which I found out when he lived in the closet beneath my stairs back in my San Francisco years. He dubbed the closet the Opium Den, spread out his sleeping bag, and grumped for five months straight about the smell in there—sour socks and smoked pot—as if he had no idea it was coming from him. I didn't mind as long as the door was closed and once a month he did the dishes.

In the envelope was a photo and a letter:

> ricket,
>   don't ask why, but my mum thought you might enjoy this picture. she's alone a lot may be why. things here knocking right along. i finally met that woman we used to dream about. feels like a different life, all this happiness.
>
>   —daryl

I gave the photo a quick glance, and my first thought was that it was some darkroom interruption, or that it had been soaked in the rain and ruined. It seemed smeared and meaningless. I didn't know why Daryl's mum—I met her years ago, briefly—thought I'd be interested in it. I tucked it into my backpack and headed for the airport, numbed by memories of Chris.

Later, when I was sitting on a bench outside of Denver's airport and waiting for my Oakland flight, an old woman with lipstick teeth approached and sat next to me. We held our boarding passes between our thighs, stared at them in silence as if they were tickets to doom. I needed distraction so I pulled the photo from my backpack.

The woman scootched toward me for a peek. "I know that sucker," she said.

"You do?"

"A picture of ice floes in Greenland," she said. "Taken from space."

"Wrong hemisphere," I said. "It's from New Zealand."

"Listen," the woman said, a bit abruptly, "you've clearly been misinformed. My nephew's neighbor risked his career to steal that photo from NASA. He was control operator for one of the first satellites sent into orbit, back in '59. Ice floes: Greenland."

"Believe what you'd like," I said.

The woman studied me, then looked at the blurred grey image in my fingers.

"No wonder," she said. "You got it held all wrong."

I turned it:

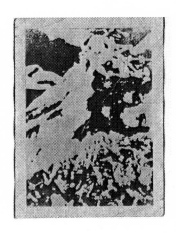

"Keep going," the woman said.

I turned it further:

"There," she said.
Recognition:

"Is that—?"
"Ain't that the question?" the woman said.
"Holy *shit*."
"Watch it," she said, pointing a feisty finger at me, "and I mean *watch it*."

❦

It's the dead of winter in New Zealand, and snowflakes stagger from a foggy Southern Cross. I take a bus through the city glow of Auckland and arrive at the train station just before midnight. I know this trip is right with neglect when above the building's giant church-like windows, across an arch of brickface, a projection of light reads

station of earth-bound ghosts

in letters eight-feet high. It seems like something I'd hallucinate or lie about, but there it is. I imagine those giant letters glowing on a woman's naked back, making me a shadow. But then my focus shifts as I realize that the sign is true: the station is closed, a hollow shell abandoned, waiting to be reborn in a spitting of trains.

There's not a soul around, so I unfold my map beneath a streetlamp and trace a path to the bus station.

Along the docks where the freightcranes live—massive mechanical birds perched in the city's misty light—my absence from Oakland begins to infect me: I left summer to sulk in winter: I left Chris in his last bites of life: I left Lori to face his funeral alone. I should be excited to be in a foreign land, but I'm not. The industrial crash of distant crates sounds to me like gunshots. Melting snow drops from the dark like beads of broken blood. I have no idea where I'm headed. No idea why I'm here.

Once I find the bus station, I sit with coffee and study Daryl's letter. Although it is postmarked from Wellington, the return address is in Tahorakuri, a small town in the center of the North Island where he grew up raising sheep. I can't imagine Daryl living anywhere but in an icy warehouse along train tracks, or in some bricken lung built beneath the city's heart. I circle the town on my map. I'll find Daryl there, I'm certain.

But the bus won't let me.

Since it's winter, the schedules aren't really scheduled. The only bus running bolts up to Cape Reinga, a fingertip of land on the top of the North Island. I scan a brochure and read that, according to tradition, Reinga is where the Maori dead go to enter the afterlife. I look at Auckland spreading everywhere in the darkness, its needle-tower injecting light into a grey dome of sky, and I wonder if Chris is alive enough to sense the betrayal of my absence—if he's alive any more at all.

It's not my destination, but I buy a ticket to Reinga anyway, because if you can't escape, you can at least eat shit where the postcards are pretty.

⚜

Cape Reinga marks a meeting place for angry seas, Tasman and South Pacific, two shades of turquoise water clashing into one. I can see the mingling of worlds, and the invisible gusts of the dead blowing through. A chubby white lighthouse marks the beginning of this life after life.

Pure white dunes shred themselves south, and I walk along the shore until the sand begins to crackle underfoot: the coast is cloaked in mollusk shells: a trillion shifting shells goggling music in the tide. The sky is grey above grey waves, as if the seas and skies have forgotten that air is not water, water is not air. It begins to rain.

A beat-up pickup truck drives toward me in the tide, spraying water, and soon a barefooted Maori couple climbs out and begins digging for their living dinner. When they begin to drive away, I stick out my thumb for kicks, and they stop for me. We find the road south.

I'm sitting in the bed of the truck, my body getting drenched but my head leaning through the window and staying dry. The two are about my age. The guy's face is full of swirling blue tattoos, and a few linger low on his wife's chubby chin. She smiles like mad and he's missing teeth all over. They tell me they're going to Auckland to check the woman into the hospital—their first baby is due in a few days.

"Giving ride to a Yankee," the guy says. He has a lifty accent that's hesherly and holy. "Least you didn't bring Jesus with you—turn us into whiteys."

I don't really know what to say, so I show him the photo.

"I seen this, mate!" he says, his gums blasting a pinkmouth grin. "My grandmother used to carry it in her purse. I think I remember it's a picture of a moth wing, blown up a thousand times? No—maybe it's the one, the ultrasound photo from Princess Diana? Farrah Fawcett, maybe it's her ultrasound?"

"You smokin' weed," the woman says.

"No, I recognize it," he says. "It's why you came all the way here?"

"I came to find a friend," I say.

"Across the world to find a friend? Man, I ain't got *no* friend like you."

"Hey," the woman says, "I'm like that with you."

"Yeah but you're my wife."

They both start laughing, poking each other's ribs and stuff. It's really something different for this world. My body is wet and icy, but my head in the cab is warm and dry.

"Lemmee see that photo," the woman says, giggling. "Farrah Fawcett's uterus."

When he hands it to her, she begins moaning loudly. At first it seems like a joke, she's so full of smiles, so her husband and I begin moaning, too.

"Helpme Lord!" he shouts. "Honky Jesus comedown!"

It's sweet and funny, the best I've felt in months, but then, surprisingly, the woman's moans shift to screams. Her husband touches her damp hair and his skin goes paler than paper. I pull the photo from her hand and stick it into my shirt pocket. In another minute, beneath her cries of pain, I hear a trickle hit the floorboards—a sound like spilling soup. We're in the middle of nowhere.

"Heybaby?" the husband says. "Heybaby?"

"I think you should speed," I say.

The rain falls, the man speeds, the woman screams: big pink screams that tear through our heads and pinch us awake. I lean in to listen as they float out the open windows and vanish with the winds of Reinga.

Three days are gone and I've landed myself in Tahorakuri, the town of Daryl's youth. Daryl's number isn't listed, but his folks' number is. If I can find their house I imagine he'll be there, sleeping in his teenaged bedroom under All Blacks rugby posters and a map of crippled America.

I feel more disconnected than ever, as if while stretched in the back of the pickup something blew through me with a pair of pruning clippers and snipped my mind free of my spine. It feels somehow good.

From the town to Daryl's family farmhouse it's a three-mile walk up a serpentine path that's more an idea of dirt than a reality of road. No one else is on this idea, and all around me the hills curve and bow, deep green with thick grass, dusted at their tops with fine puffs of snow. A rusty tractor sinks in the mud. Sheep blot the landscape, and from far away they look like golf balls eating grass. I concentrate on counting the sheep because every few seconds I look around and get this chumpslap feeling of being in a different hemisphere instead of in the hospital room with my dying friend.

Wait.

There are 60-million sheep in this country and 3-million people. For every person in this country there are 20 sheep. For every sheep in this country there is $1/20^{th}$ of a person, and if the average person in New Zealand weighs 141 pounds, and the average sheep weighs only 83, and if one considers the collective consumption of both calories and natural resources, it then follows that:

I am not worth my weight in sheep.

Even so, 20 of them belong to me, and I've come to take what's mine.

I walk between a pair of broken fenceposts and begin selecting my sheep. Only it's hard to do so without a gun or tranquilizer darts, so I begin yelling *at* sheep and then I'm yelling *with* sheep, top of my lungs, and before I know it I'm chasing sheep with tears falling from my face and Daryl's mum is chasing sheep with me.

Daryl's mum?

I like people who are so polite that you don't have to explain anything, just tell them that you're a really tight friend of their son Daryl and they give you a hankie for your drizzles and offer you his bedroom. With dinner simmering, Mum makes a big pot of tea and tells me that Daryl is down in Wellington these days.

"He's incredibly happy," she says, "things are going brilliantly, really."

"That's what I hear," I say.

"He told you about Sally?" she says.

"If that's his dream-woman, yes—he mentioned her in his letter."

"And he sent you the photograph?"

"Yeah, I wanted to ask—"

"I certainly didn't expect you so soon," she says.

"I was going to ask—"

"Later," she says, rather sternly, then leans forward and stares at my shirt. A pink stain shaped like a ghost is smeared down its front, left over from my trip to Reinga. "What on earth is all over you?"

"Placenta," I say.

"Good lord," she says, "maybe you should change."

"I wish."

A pursed look of disgust crinkles through Mum's face as she turns away and stares into her ashtray. Now that I can smell her—rose oil and mud—I vaguely remember her visiting Daryl in San Francisco years ago. It seems like she was only in our apartment for five minutes. Big green eyes, I remember those, but otherwise it's as if I'm sitting with a schoolmarm ghost. Her hair falls to her waist in a straight white gush, and she wears a rolled black veil atop her head. Though her hands are webbed with veins of age, something in her is jumpy, like a child playing jax.

"So the Mister must be out, what?" I say. "Shepherding?"

"No, no," she says. "We have people for that. He's in the basement drinking."

"That's good," I say.

She covers me in smoke.

"Go tell him supper's on," she says.

In the basement, there is a chair and a basement. Daryl's dad is drinking in it, the chair in the basement. His beard is flecked with dandruff. Drippy bits crowd the corners of his eyes. Something down here smells like a delivery room, but that might be me.

When I introduce myself, I see that he holds small scissors against his toes.

"I'd shake your hand," he solemnly says, "but mine's full of toenails."

"Food's on."

Over dinner, I tell Daryl's folks that I work in a bookshop in Denver, just so it doesn't seem like I'm a no-good bum. They don't seem fooled.

"Show Ricket the bloody book rooms," Daryl's dad says through a volcano of corn.

"It wouldn't hurt you," Mum says to him, "to climb those stairs yourself."

Daryl's dad shoots a look at her, then gazes into his glass of whiskey.

"Either way," I say, pretending not to notice the tension I've brought into the room.

"If you like mysteries and westerns," Mum says, "there're loads up there. Myself, I collect romance."

Dad stands sharply from the table, causing a fork to fall to the floor. He stares at it for a moment, then, with a morose snort, walks toward the cellar stairs. When the door closes behind him, Mum pours a splash of whiskey into my glass.

"That's the most we've spoken all year," she says.

With a little grunt, I begin bringing the dinner mess to the sink. I don't want to get involved in these domestic depressions—I'm here to track down Daryl—and I've already decided that as soon as heavenly possible, I'm out the door.

When I turn to gather the next round of dishes, Daryl's mum is standing behind me, a crazed glaze in her eyes. I very nearly scream.

"Leave those," she says, "and come with me."

Mum's book room is a third-floor turret of wall-to-wall novels. The shelves reach high up to the ceiling, and although the books are neatly stacked and sorted, their spines are cracked and dusty. As far as I can tell, the mysteries and westerns cover one wall, and romance spans the rest. Oddly placed between the shelves are knick-knacks suitable for a curiosity cabinet: jars holding floating snakes, necklaces stitched with teeth, old bottles crammed with human hair. An autographed photo of Johnny Cash biting his lip and flipping the bird hangs above the door. The room's only furniture is a simple little chair and teatable, perched before a window that looks out over dreaming sheep. Near a solitary lamp, I see a tiny square cut into a wall stained by nicotine. I pull the photograph from my back pocket and hold it against the smoky frame. It fits.

"This is where it went?" I say.

"Quite observant," she says, putting out a cigarette. "Next question."

"Is this the question game?"

"The interrogation game," she says.

For a moment, I stare into the deep grey swirls of the photo in my hand. Shadows slash through everything.

"I don't even know where to begin," I say. "All of this—being here. My friend, Chris, he's dying. Dead maybe."

"People die, Ricket," she says, seemingly unconcerned. She walks along the shelves packed with romance, and her thoughts trail off as she strums her fingers down the spines. *Devil in a Tux. Cowpoke Summer.* "The last time an American stood in this room," she finally says. "He might very well have appeared in any one of these stories, Ricket. A true hero, he was, worthy of emulation."

"Neat," I say, creeped by her drift. "Maybe I can get Daryl's address before I go?"

"This will be of interest to you," she says, "trust me. His name was Skadgett, this American drifter, and a few years before Daryl was born he rode up the road on a barebacked horse. Looking for work, he was, for a place to sleep and work. He was a heavy-headed cowboy—chaps and furs and all the rest—a bearded man who reeked of woodsmoke and meat. He spoke very little, and carried in his rucksack all the tokens of his travels: a shrunken head, a monkey's paw, an ear in a baby-food jar—things you might otherwise find in a nightmare. It might seem difficult to believe right now, but my husband and I were deeply in love back then, enriched each day by laughter. We thought Skadgett inconceivably strange at first, frightening even, but gradually came to embrace him. He stayed much longer than even he ex-pected. He blew through here and changed everything."

"A stranger comes to town," I say, motioning to the walls of books. "Like a romance, like a western."

"And yes, Ricket," she says, gesturing to the sinister collectibles perched between their spines, "like a mystery. During the years that he stayed here, Skadgett lived in an outbuilding beyond these pastures. A dark, simple man, and it seems inconceivable in retrospect, but he and my husband grew into a deep friend-ship. Best friends, you might even say, inseparable in their drinks and cards and heavy work. All was well for quite some time."

My eyes skim the shelves, and out of my own discomfort, I retrieve a book and absently flip through its pages.

"And this Skadgett—he's been gone a long time?"

"Years ago," she says casually, "murdered."

"Murdered?" I say.

Mum taps the stained frame on the wall.

"The photograph," I say.

"Patience," Mum says curtly, then pauses to light a cigarette. "You do know, Ricket, how deeply Daryl values your friend-ship?"

"This is about Daryl then."

"It is," she says, "it isn't." She pauses to grind her jaw, and her behavior grows as disturbing as her words: she adjusts a taxi-dermed bat until it is aligned perfectly between romance novels; she retrieves a faded tube of chapstick from a shelf and cakes it on her thin lips; she stares longingly out the window. "Lis-ten," she continues. "About a year before wee Daryl was born, my husband and Skadgett and I took a week in the winter and rented a clubhouse on the west coast of the South Island—a mystic, sleepy town named Otirako. If you can call it a town. Not even a pub there, no shops, and we spent most of our time walking far down the beaches and deep into the rainforest, shar-ing bottles, playing games by the woodstove. On one of those walks, Skadgett and I separated ourselves from my husband and made like bandits back to the clubhouse. We'd been drinking all morning and it was all but inevitable, the two of us, that at some point we would—"

"You and Skadgett were snogging," I say.

"You must know by now," she says abruptly, "that these things happen with adults, Ricket. Of course they are unforgivable, but somehow they still happen. There is no justification for betrayal, but perhaps now, being here, you can imagine the isolation I felt. The loneliness brought on by those we love."

I think of course of Chris, of Lori, of friendships lost.

"Isolation is not geographical," I say.

"You see, Ricket?" she continues. "You and I have more in common than one might first think. And I'm sure you know the rest: back at the clubhouse, Skadgett and I had enjoyed each other too slowly, and my husband came in looking for us, all

giggles and drinks and hoorah-hey. Found Skadgett and I together on the floor, our bodies puzzled together like a single
slippery beast. We were baffled by the choice we'd made but
powerless to change it. We didn't even try to explain, just paused
inside each other and closed our eyes and waited for something
to happen. Something certainly did: slowly, my husband walked
round the clubhouse until he found a hunting rifle perched on
the wall. Carefully, he checked for bullets and peered down its
barrel. Promptly, he stepped our way and opened fire. Skadgett
was heroic. Stayed pressed on top of me, sheltering me with
his body, as three bullets burned through his back. I could feel
their force thumping against my chest, knocking the wind out
of me. Skadgett died inside of me, eyes opened, and I thought
I was dead as well. When my husband asked me to stand up,
Skadgett's blood and sweat covering my naked front, I thought
for a moment he would kill me next. But he didn't. Instead he
began to cry, and to be frank, I don't believe he has ever stopped.
He stepped forward that day and embraced me. I was alive, you
see. Filled with betrayal, but alive."

She touches her hair compulsively, adjusting the veil that sits
awkwardly atop her head.

"My husband and I didn't speak a word," she continues, "but
together, after nightfall, we dragged Skadgett's body up to a
clifftop cemetery that overlooked the beach. There, silently, we
buried his remains inside the grave of a little boy. Blended their
bones as if old age and young were one."

"No one knows this?" I say.

"There were no inquiries or detectives, if that's what you
mean. Once Skadgett was buried, there seemed to be no reason
to speak of it again. Of course our silence ate our relationship
alive, but the incident seemed inexplicable, beyond words, and
months later, back here at home, images of the South Island

herself seemed to offer the only answer for our behavior: tangled brush, crashing waves, shadows lurking in small town doorways. A strange occurrence in a strange town on a strange island—that seemed to be all the explanation we needed."

"That's it then," I say, eyeing the exit.

"But that's not it," she says. For a moment she digs a polished nail into the back of her scalp, like she's shimmying beneath a hidden scab. "As it would happen, about nine months from the day of Skadgett's murder—"

"Daryl."

"Yes: Daryl was born. The timing of this did not go unnoticed, nor did the undeniable resemblance, as he grew older, between our little boy and our dead Skadgett. Of course, like Skadgett's murder, my husband and I never spoke about it. And to make matters even murkier, a few weeks after Daryl's birth, I'd brought in a roll of film to have developed—baby pictures, you know? *The Happy Family Leaves the Hospital. The Newborn Infant Sits with Daddy.* And there, sandwiched between snapshots of Daryl's earliest hours, was the photo you now hold. It looked like nothing at first, a mishap of light and dark—perhaps, I thought, a misaligned glimpse of the checkerboard linoleum on the delivery room floor. It wasn't until much later, years even, when I was sorting through the negatives, that I'd realized this was the first photo ever taken of our little Daryl. He would have been minutes old. Eyes still closed."

"Do I want to know this?" I say.

"Not everything is about you, Ricket."

As I consider this, Mum carries a dustbunny to the window.

"And your husband?" I say. "What's he think of all this?"

"He's never said a word about the photo," she says, "even when he spotted it between snapshots of our newborn Daryl. Maybe he's never examined it closely, the way some of us have. You think my husband's miserable now, with his cellar and his drinks, just imagine if—this is another matter for silence, Ricket."

"Why send me the photo?" I say. "And why tell me any of this? We met for five minutes ten years ago and you were probably unimpressed."

"Very," she says. "I needed to take a shower the moment I left your apartment. Poor Daryl, living in your little closet like a hiding child. But to answer your question: look around you, and what do you see?"

"Romance novels," I say, speaking of needing showers.

"What else?"

"A house in the middle of nowhere. Sheep. Isolation."

"Like living in a grave," she says, sighing. "I have nothing but time, loneliness and time. Perhaps my husband and I should have left each other instead of silently sharing these miseries. But, despite my unforgivable actions with Skadgett, I have honored our vows of marriage. Friendship, even."

"That doesn't answer my question," I say. "Why me?"

"When you are at home, Ricket, what do you see?"

An image comes to mind: "Kitchen knives," I say, "covered in lotion and blood."

"Foul," she says with a wince.

"I also see a best friend shot in the face."

"I'll tell you what else," she says. "When you are at home, Ricket, you see a place you want to leave."

Her accuracy stuns me into a stutter. "Not," I say, "always. Sometimes home can be really—homey."

"I've forwarded to Daryl, from you, eight postcards from eight countries in three years. Now, let me repeat: home is a place you want to leave, yes?"

Freak.

"This," she says, "wherever this is, is a place you want to leave *to*. All you ever need is a half-baked reason—"

"A blurry savior," I say. "A Cracker Jack ghost."

"The photo could be of anyone, Ricket. Anything."

"But who do you think it is?"

"In the right light," she says, "it looks to me like Skadgett, but I suppose it doesn't matter. What matters is that I've stared at it and felt—what? Felt myself change under his gaze. Felt comforted. Yes, I think it's him. But then I spend too much time alone."

"I'm still not sure why I'm here," I say.

"I have something I need done. A favor. Don't worry, it'll suit you."

"I think I'll leave now," I say, feeling duped.

"It involves bones," she says, tapping ashes to the floor.

"Bones?"

"Human, old, dead: yes, bones."

"Well then," I say, biting on my guilty lip, "I guess I'm in."

❧

In Wellington, Daryl answers his apartment door in a tattered bathrobe, overweight, balding, looking grey in the jowls and positively haggard. It's been nearly a decade since we've seen each other, and he resembles nothing less than a hungover corpse. Adding to his miserable appearance, a split-lipped cat yawns in his arms. My immediate reaction is to consider how he and his mother have been able to call his present condition *happy*. He drags off a home-rolled cig, squints a little, then turns to walk inside. "Ricket," he says in his drollest voice, "color me frightened."

When I first met Daryl in San Francisco, he'd been sleeping in the park and working in the Chinese deli up the street from my apartment. He was frazzled and burnt, but joyfully so, and I took him in, offered him my closet, intending to let him collect himself for a few weeks. Two years later—the last time we talked—he left my closet to work on a fishing rig in Alaska. Last I heard, he'd sliced open his leg while scaling vats of tuna, nearly bled to death on the boat, and was deported right out of the emergency room in Juno.

"You're a hard one to find," I say as we take our seats on the couch.

Daryl seems intent on ignoring this. Rather than respond, he studies my shirt.

"What's on your shirt?"

"Placenta."

"Freaky," he says.

I'm weary from traveling, so Daryl's laconic nature is welcome. Sitting here with him I'm reminded of our friendship, the hours we spent digging into each other's thoughts on couches far more rancid than this one. That was the past, though, and this Daryl's flat looks like it's clipped from the pages of an interior design magazine. Everything is stark and minimalist, precisely matched—hardly what I was expecting, given my memories of him and his present state of sloth.

"By the way," I say, "remember Chris, big smiley guy from Oaktown?"

"Sure," he says. "Let me guess: married, four kids, trailer park in Bakersfield."

"Close," I say, "he was murdered."

As the afternoon creeps forward, Daryl sits in silence and seems tormented by the fog boiling against the outside of his living room window. The view from his apartment shows downtown Wellington as a colorful blur beneath the fog. Deco buildings curve around the bay, cradled by lush green hills. Next to the window is a framed cover of *L* magazine with a woman half-dressed on its cover. The photo is crisp with clarity.

"Who's this?" I say.

"Sally," he says, rather glumly. "Fiancée."

"She looks—"

"Bleedin' perfect is what," he somberly says.

Daryl seems so upset that I change the subject.

"I got Skad—that picture," I say.

"Yeah, sorry about that," he says. "My mum's nuts."

"I slept in your bed."

"You what?"

"They've got quite a set-up," I say, "your folks. They gave me your address, cooked me a few meals. We had some chats."

Daryl lights a cigarette off the one burning in his fingers.

"Chats," he says, "for real? Dad too?"

"Small chats."

"Strange," he says. "I don't think I've had a chat with Dad since I was—scratch that. I've *never* had a chat with my dad. Maybe about cricket once—does that count?"

"Your mum told me you've turned your life around," I say, trying to cheer him up. "*Happiness*, I think she used that word."

"Yes," he says, "I reckon *happy* is the right word. Everything's wonderful, yes."

And for a split second he's convincing, then he breaks down bawling on my chest, adding anguish to my stains.

Daryl and I have been walking through Wellington for a few days now, disappearing into basement bars at night, roaming the dockyards during the day. We spend some afternoons—like this one—sitting on mossy docks, watching the boats clack against each other along the waterfront. As we reconnect it occurs to me that, for all the appearance of change, Daryl is the same: he's still not happy unless he's miserable. This feels somehow encouraging.

As a young boy chases a boppy red ball along the water's edge, Daryl tells me that my arrival has made his life infinitely better. I find this hard to believe, because I've been feeling like a roaming cadaver. I have a secret, too, thanks to his mum, and though it periodically stifles me into uneasy lulls, Daryl doesn't seem to notice. He's called in sick to his design firm each day, and he hasn't returned Sally's calls. I still haven't met her, but once, while Daryl was showering, the phone rang and it was her. We had a nice long talk.

"I need to go to the South Island," I say, "vanish for a spell."

"I'm keen," he says. "When do we leave?"

"I think you should get back to work before they sack you. Get back in synch with Sally. I've been here three days and I'm already ruining your life, Daryl."

"Don't flatter yourself, Ricket—my life's been shit for years. Work won't even fire me. They say I'm an *inspiration* to the other designers." Daryl is truly bothered by this. He sinks his head in his hands and the word *inspiration* blows over us from the briny waves of the bay. "Sally really *loves* me."

"Isn't that a good thing?" I say.

"It's incredible, yes, all of it." He slams his palms into his head so his dark hair rattles. "Perfect paychecks, perfect coffees, perfect lotions—mice behind the walls, mate. Cavities." He touches the front of my shirt. For some reason this changes his gears. "The other day," he says, "did you say 'placenta'?"

"Yeah."

"Thought so," he says. He contemplates the waves. "Placenta: now that's bloody inspirational."

※

For the past week we've been skirting around the South Island. The land expresses itself in some wildness beyond words, seems a dream dug from the subconscious of the earth. As we drive, the landscape morphs from beach to rainforest to alpine peaks. Bathtubs and wagons grow sideroad grass. There's hardly a soul except lurking figures in tiny towns, and I'm beginning to understand Skadgett's story: the way this ancient island might blur one's allegiance to others.

There are no signs for Otirako, just a skinny road that winds through giant ferns and mantles of rain. When we arrive it's dusk. Weeping trees halt in a cragland of rocks, rocks halt in a sandland of grey, sand halts in the blackland of the crashing Tasman Sea. A shack on stilts sits in a lagoon, a white heron sits on the shack. Everything flows together under a glucose fog. With all the blends of grey, if I make my hands into a box and point the box out into the waves, it looks not unlike a photograph I once saw.

Standing barefoot in the tide, Daryl tells me that he's always dreamed of moving down to the South Island, but he's never been in this region, and never heard of Otirako.

"Someone recommended it," I say.

When night overwhelms, we walk from the beach into town, a half-dozen shacks boxed around a tiny war memorial. That's it—not a shop, not a bar, and all the lights are off. The darkness is inconceivable. We stand on the vacant sidewalk, a slatted thing made of wood, and listen for voices. There are none.

From a few shacks down a burly woman comes walking, slicing the darkness with a flashlight. She wears knee-high gumboots and a skirt stitched with roses. When she reaches us she says, "Looking for me, then?"

Without knowing it, we were. She takes us past a toolshed and back to a broken barn that's been remodeled into a clubhouse. It's a palace of clutter and knick-knacks, souvenirs from

All Blacks rugby games, a century's worth of photos and obitu-
aries tacked to the walls. Hunting and fishing gear hangs from
cobwebbed antlers. In the back are two tiny rooms with mattresses on the floor. The old woman gives us spuds and bangers
and a pot to cook them in, and shows us a little fridge holding
bottles of Speight's Ale. She disappears before we think to thank
her.

"*Drink Speight's, Lose Yer Mates*," Daryl says. "That's the slo-
gan."

"Sally should be here tomorrow," I say.

"Wait—*Sally* should?"

"She asked where she might meet us. I said here, in Otirako—"

"She asked when?" Daryl says.

I haven't really thought about it, but now I feel like I've be-
trayed him somehow.

"Last week she called, when you were in the shower. I told her
we'd be here. If she wants to meet up, y'know?"

"Want a Speight's?" Daryl says.

I must've fallen asleep, because when I open my eyes it's past
midnight and I'm alone. An empty mug sits in my lap, a cold
wind raps the window panes.

Last night, Daryl and I sat side by side, remembering the
early days of our friendship. He mentioned how easily we've
fallen back into it. Later, he found a big Bible-looking book that
held doodles and messages from all the folks who've stayed here
in the past. When I dozed off, he was still reading it. Now he
snores beyond the walls.

My socks are wet with some earlier rain. I pour myself a beer
and look at the photo again. I keep expecting it to change, to
begin opening and closing its eyes like some Cracker Jack trick,

or to reveal something I need to know. I keep expecting myself to change under its gaze, but I don't. I guess we don't know until later about change.

Daryl's bedsprings squeak, followed by a rumble of snores. Soon, a young woman walks out of the bedroom and closes the door behind her. She's beautiful, tall and spindly, and sleep traipses through her braids. She wears only a GrapeApe tee-shirt and socks—slightly more clothing than in the magazine photo of her that hangs on Daryl's wall. I freeze when she slaps my knees and sits on the floor near my feet.

"Sally," she says.

"I gathered. How long I been asleep?"

"Few hours," she says.

"Feels like a lifetime."

For a moment we soak each other in. Between my fingers, the photo waits.

"Choice," she says, "that's that photo?" I must look puzzled because she adds, "Daryl told me you were on some quest."

"Some quest is on me," I say.

I hand her the image—it seems blurrier now, passing between our hands.

"I *know* this picture," she says.

Calmly, Sally tells me that it's a magnified image of a French intelligence agent's thumbprint. The guy was part of the team of spies who, in 1985, blew up the *Rainbow Warrior*, a Greenpeace boat docked in Auckland's harbor. She tells me the boat was destroyed by the French government to prevent it from blockading nuclear testing in the Pacific, and that a photographer died in the explosion.

"How's that?" she says. "Another layer for you: bloody Frenchies getting away with murder."

"It doesn't really clarify anything, but thanks."

"Maybe it's not supposed to be clear," she says, handing me back the photo. She leans in close. "What's on yer shirt?"

"Placenta."

"Looks like an island," she says. "Can I smell it?"

"No," I say. But she tries to anyway, furious with play, and ends up biting me softly on the wrist. I push her away and try to pretend that she hasn't turned my spine into a shivering blowtorch. "Daryl asleep?" I say.

"Bloody rock."

"Well then," I say, "you wanna help me dig up a body?"

She searches for the joke, but it's just not here.

"You're serious," she whispers, looking toward Daryl's snores. She touches her tee-shirt. "I can't wear this, I'll freeze. I have to get my clothes."

"It's a secret."

For a moment, she considers this.

"How close are you and Daryl?" she says.

"We don't have much time."

Sally looks around the clubhouse, then untacks one of the All Blacks uniforms from the wall—rugby shorts and shirt—and climbs into it. Cobwebs dance along her shoulder as she digs a pair of fishing boots from the closet.

"Shall we exhume?" she says.

۱۷

The Otirako cemetery is a garden of mossy tombstones planted on a grassy cliff high above the beach. On our way here, Sally and I stopped by the toolshed for flashlights and shovels. She doesn't seem surprised by what we're about to do, like she's ready to simply trust me—maybe because I'm Daryl's friend. I like the fact that we walk together in silence, that she's okay with not complicating this desecration with words.

It doesn't take long to find the little boy's grave. His stone is small and angelic, and jumbled with rusty toys. Sally and I silently position our flashlights and begin to dig. The earth dispels herself with softness. A few hours later, Sally lowers me into the hole, and I crouch atop the lid of the boy's small coffin. It creaks beneath my weight as I plunge my hands into the rooty earth and begin to gather Skadgett's tumbled bones.

Skadgett has seen better nights. His skin and flesh are gone, and the skeleton that remains is blemished with lichen-like growths. Many of his bones are held together by rotten furs, and as I hoist him out to lay him in the grass his head pops off like a skull-on-a-spring. Sally scoops it up and fakes a rugby kick. This makes me laugh.

As Sally scoops dirt back into the dead boy's hole, I grab Skadgett and make a halfass sack from his furs. I drag him down the path and over the beach. I take him into the tide and as the smell of his death is rinsed away by waves, I see some moonlight Sally up on the clifftop, shaking her arms madly and laughing at my poor bath-giving skills. I don't have practice, but some day I might be good.

When Skadgett is clean, I begin to cram his bones into my backpack. As I'm doing so, I check the acrid pockets of his furs, thinking that whatever Daryl's mum is after must be in them. I expect to find some decaying love letter or a map written in blood, but except for the husks of bugs, his pockets are empty. I wonder if Mum will be disappointed.

The sunrise begins though the sun still hides. Sally joins me on the beach. Leaning over my shoulder, she smells like booze and roots.

"Daryl will be awake soon," I say. "We should go."

As I'm carrying Skadgett on my back, creeping down the path

and watching the bounce of Sally's back, I begin to feel as if a cloud has clustered around me. Life seems ugly, friendships fragile. As I'm sulking in this, Sally suddenly stops in the middle of an arch of silver ferns. She turns and faces me. She is beautiful and her eyelids tell me she is beautiful, and waiting here the weight is on my back but she holds all the grace. She inches toward me and this place booms with primal life, and I want nothing less than to do what my body is silently asking me to disturb.

She reaches for my hands. She tries to kiss me.

I wonder if Chris, in his final moments of life, held the hands of a stranger—a doctor, a janitor, a lonely nurse—and under his opiated veils believed they were my own: my hands, guiding him past the garbage cans on his way out the dark and final door.

Sally tries, but I don't.

Shortly after Sally sneaks back to bed, Daryl crawls out of the shower and begins making coffee. I haven't yet slept.

"I think your placenta is starting to reek," Daryl says, whiffing the clubhouse air.

"It's probably just my stuff," I say. I carry my backpack across the room. When I set it in the grass outside the door, the man inside clacks against himself.

"I met Sally," I say.

"She's not bashful," Daryl says.

"She's really the woman you've always dreamed about?"

"The one my dreams dreamed for me," he says. "Bloody angelic."

He walks toward me with two cups of coffee, and in the middle of the room he stops. He gets a thinking frown going, and grouches the floor a bit with his eyes.

"I read that guest book for a bit last night," he says. "Small country."

"How so?"

"Just that my folks came here to stay one time. Before I was born, they did, in this very clubhouse. I bloody well may have been conceived on that nasty couch right there. Of course they never mentioned it to me."

"I thought they never told you anything," I say.

"I'll have to ask them sometime is what I mean."

Daryl reaches out to hand me a coffee, and here, in this simple moment, our hands touch. It really is only a moment, but there's a reminder in the warmth of our contact that blood flows beneath our skin. We are alive, both of us, and friends. For some reason, though I know it will wrench his mind into misery, I think about telling Daryl all that I know about his mum and Skadgett: that his whole life he's been wrong about his father being the silent wastrel drinking in the cellar; that his real father was murdered in the very moment of Daryl's conception; that his real father is right now trapped in a bag of bones on the other side of the door.

But, for the moment, I enjoy my silence instead. I enjoy the way this secret feels, bumping around inside of me, looking for a way out. I keep it inside because no person, no matter who, deserves to know such things. It could ruin even the most perfect life.

"Daryl," I say, "I've got something you need to know."

Daryl reacts just as I thought he would: he thinks I've made it all up. I don't show him Skadgett's bones or try to prove him wrong because I know that once I'm gone he'll smell the seriousness of my words. He changes the subject to memories we share—lost now to lost time—and we share a morning of coffee and talk, just the two of us, just like we used to. When Sally wakes up, she immediately finds Daryl's lap and begins kissing his bald spot. Uncomfortably, I tell them that I'm stepping out for a walk on the beach. After quietly gathering my pack from outside the door, I sneak away from Otirako and begin the trip to Auckland to catch a plane home.

On the way, I have every intention of delivering Skadgett's bones to Mum's smoky romance room, as arranged, for her to shelve between her books and cherish during lonely nights. But when the train stops in Tahorakuri, I don't get off. Instead, I click toward Auckland with Skadgett rattling my backpack—a date, perhaps, for the blow-up doll left yawning on my Denver couch.

But I won't make it as far as home: the customs police will surely catch me trying to smuggle his remains out of New Zealand. They'll upend my bag and Skadgett will pour out, his bones clanging against a shiny metal table top.

When the police ask for my identification, I'll tell them that I have none.

When they persist, I'll show them the photograph. And maybe, instead of locking me in a room to contemplate all the wrongs I've done, they'll squint into the infinite smears of grey and find me—adequate and forgiven—somewhere hidden inside.

Finalists

∞ *Girl* ∞

CHERYL ALU

Charlotte was five years old when she changed her name to Jeffrey. At first everyone was amused. Her parents. The other parents, and the kids at her school. Even her teachers. Everyone said it with a smile. But Charlotte was serious. She wouldn't answer to anything other than Jeffrey, and for some time that's what almost everybody called her. It was just easier.

But still. There had been many long discussions at the dinner table and sitting on the edge of her bed when both her parents, together and separately, would appeal to her common sense. That's just the way it was, they told her. She was a girl and Jeffrey was a boy's name. Charlotte would nod in agreement and then look up from under the bill of a baseball cap or a leather headband and say that she knew it was a boy's name because there were two Jeffries in her class. As a compromise they offered the nickname Charlie, but that only resulted in a long explanation of what it meant to compromise.

The parents were advised, by people who knew about these things, that this was a phase and it would pass. In the meantime they tried bribery. They bought her everything she wanted: trucks, dinosaurs, camouflage cargo pants, and everything they wanted her to want: dolls, tea sets, jewelry making kits, and dresses. She gave them false hope when she showed an interest in one of the dolls. It was the G.I. Jane doll but, nevertheless, they were willing to take what they could get.

They tried issuing orders, but that felt wrong. They tried indifference but that was too hard to fake. Then they tried something called Family Yoga. It was supposed to be a relaxing and bonding experience for the family, but mostly it was a way for them to be together without having to talk. Charlotte liked doing the poses and made friends with a boy named Sam.

The teacher was a young woman from India who had dark eyes that seemed to never blink and dusty skin that complimented the gold she wore. She might have been barely twenty and her name was Diane. That was her American name she said. She wanted her life to be all American now. She sat in perfect lotus and smiled at the parents and children from the little carpeted platform in front of the class where candles and incense burned to the left and right of her. At each session the mother couldn't help feeling everything was going to be fine. But that feeling never lasted long enough.

Soon the father became impatient with Charlotte and her name change. He hated that she wore only boy's clothes and played with trucks and molded plastic monsters and Bionicle Legos. It was becoming tiresome. It was defeating him. The mother told him about a girl she knew in college who had a boy's name. She was called Michael. She was very smart and clever and she traveled all over the world and now she lives in Vienna and was the curator of a museum or an art gallery or maybe it was an art auction house. But her husband had left the room before she'd finished this story and she wasn't really sure what point she was trying to make.

—

On the way home from Family Yoga, when he just couldn't take it anymore, he stopped the car and turned around in his seat to look at Charlotte. He said without emotion that there would be no more of this Jeffrey crap. Her name was Charlotte and that was what she would be called. No more Jeffrey. End of story. While Charlotte listened to her father she felt in the pocket of her jacket for the smooth piece of green glass she had found several days ago. She knew it was probably just a hunk of old beer bottle but it was the color of the ocean and had specks of sand and pinpoints of air suspended inside. She lived in the very center of the country and had never seen the ocean. She waited for her father to finish talking and decided not to say anything. It didn't matter to her anymore what she was called. It only mattered to her father. So she let Jeffrey go.

When Charlotte was almost six her dolls began to die. At first, her parents were happy that she showed any interest at all in the dolls she had always ignored. Her mother would dust around them and rearrange them and try to convince herself that Charlotte noticed or cared. Now, at dinner or just before going to sleep, she would matter-of-factly announce that Carol or Wendy wasn't feeling well. Then, a day or two later, she would tell her parents that Carol or Wendy or whoever had died. The parents were torn between being excited that she was actually playing with dolls (she's named them!) and being disturbed that it took such morbid form. Once a doll had been declared dead, she would put it in a box under her bed. Her parents refused to buy replacements, hoping she'd revive the ones who had "died." But Charlotte didn't seem to miss them. More like relieved that they were gone. Her parents stopped discussing the dolls, glad to be through with all the talk of death.

Charlotte's teacher called to complain about Charlotte using the boys' restroom again and this time the mother could only respond with a tired sigh. This bathroom problem was an on again off again thing with Charlotte that never seemed to get resolved. She would simply begin using the boy's bathroom and then, arbitrarily, when she felt her point had been made, she'd go back to using the girls' facility. After a while when the matter had been forgotten about, she'd start using the boys' room again. The mother had read dozens of parenting books and had spoken with many experts and none of it had ever been of any help whatsoever. When it came to her daughter the rules seemed not to apply. She suggested to the teacher that if she had any ideas she was welcome to try them. The teacher said that taking away a favorite toy sometimes works.

"We tried that once," her mother said. "We took away a doll and when we gave it back to her it died."

"Excuse me?"

"Charlotte said the doll felt sad, and then the doll felt sick, and then the doll died. She put it in the box under her bed with all the other dead dolls. The ones who've died, I mean. We've stopped buying her dolls now and to tell you the truth, I think she's happy about that." The mother realized her voice was sounding unusually shrill and so she stopped speaking.

"I see," said the teacher.

After nine months of Family Yoga the mother began to notice that the musky smell of the incense Diane burned seemed to have followed them home. It permeated the house. The pillows on her bed and her husband's good white dress shirts that he wore to work somehow—impossibly—smelled of Family Yoga incense. One rainy Wednesday evening in the yoga studio when all the children were eager and wobbly, the men hesitant and stiff-limbed, and all the women wore the same helpless smile, it occurred to the mother that her husband was incapable of executing a pose without Diane touching him. Dark slender fingers tracing his spine to correct his posture. A palm pressed to his solar plexus to regulate his breathing. A hand touching the top of his head to focus his concentration. She tried to do Fire In The Belly breathing but the thick sweet smell of the incense and flowers was making her sick.

The next week the mother didn't go to Family Yoga with her husband and daughter. She still did the deep breathing awareness exercise and the mind centering exercise but she did them in her car, parked across the street from the studio where she watched the door and waited for the class to be over. Our minds are restless monkeys, she remembered Diane saying. We must acquire stillness. Like the pole in the center of the monkey cage, yoga is a place to stop.

Then the mother watched the three of them leave the studio and enter the ice cream shop two doors down: her daughter, her husband, and the young Indian woman who wanted to give American minds a place to stop. She watched as they disappeared into the crowd inside the shop, then the mother got out of her car and walked to her husband's car that was parked nearby. She put two coins into the parking meter because his time was almost up. Then she got back into her own car and drove home.

Charlotte had begun to pray. Her parents weren't religious people and had never mentioned prayers to her so it came as a bit of surprise when they heard her in her room talking to someone. They stood outside her door and listened. They heard her say

"Please, dear God," and they knew she was praying. They heard her say, "Please dear God, make my penis grow." Neither one of the parents wanted to tackle that problem. All they could manage in that moment was a wordless search of each other's face. The next morning at breakfast they exchanged nervous glances, each hoping the other would find a way to talk about this odd prayer. But Charlotte was the first to bring it up, in a way, by announcing that when she grew up and became a boy, she wanted to be a fireman. Her mother was quick to point out that girls can be fire... can fight fires too. Her father, feeling that his wife had missed the point, took Charlotte's arm to get her attention and told her that when she grew up she would still be a girl. Not a boy. Then she would be a woman. Not a man. Charlotte met his straightforward gaze and waited until he released her arm. Then she said, "But after my penis grows—then I'll be a boy."

The next Wednesday her husband was away on a business trip. Two nights in another town. The mother knew Diane would ask about him as she always did whenever he missed a class. But that evening, when she entered the studio, someone called Simon was sitting in a perfect lotus on the little stage. He smiled and kept his eyes closed while everyone found a space to unfold their yoga mats and fold up their legs into a mirror image of the master. Then Simon opened his clear clean-living eyes and said, "Welcome." She couldn't tell if the ringing sound came from inside her head or outside the studio. The whole place smelled different too. Simon had great clumps of jasmine incense burning and the pale blue smoke made her eyes water.

The wardrobe wars began again when Charlotte was invited to Sam's birthday party and her father insisted she wear a dress— the dress he had brought back from his trip as a gift for her.

Charlotte hadn't worn anything with a skirt since she was old enough to dress herself, and she and her mother had thought the matter of clothes was now a given.

"Why," said the mother to the father, "are you doing this?"

"Because somebody has to. And you don't seem to be interested."

But why, she wanted to say, were they not discussing something more relevant; like the reason he ate all of the left over Chinese food when he knew they were planning to share it for dinner? Or why weren't they talking about that night they went to the movies and while she was in the lobby buying popcorn he gave away her seat saying that he thought she had found a better one? And why has he stopped answering his cell phone? But they weren't going to talk about any of that because now he was hammering away at all the reasons why it was important that their daughter wear a dress.

Meanwhile, Charlotte went to her room and quietly cut the dress into pink and yellow pieces with her mother's pinking shears. She stood in the center of the jagged scraps of cloth that looked like a party had died and heard her father leave the house, slamming the door as hard as he could. Charlotte didn't go to Sam's after all. Instead, she tried to copy a picture of a whale from a book while her mother took a hot bath and the whole house smelled like eucalyptus.

Punishment wasn't a word they liked to use but her behavior had to be dealt with—playdates were canceled, entire Saturdays were spent in her room, her favorite cookies stayed in the bag and grew stale, she missed episodes of Sponge Bob. There were more long talks at the dinner table during which both parents suffered a loss of appetite while Charlotte ate everything on her plate. She knew, by now, not to even ask for dessert. Nothing was settled. No decisions were made. It became unclear who was punishing whom. Charlotte continued to wear the boy's clothes that occupied half of her closet and continued to ignore the other half—the dresses with matching socks, the skirts with petticoats attached and the pink pants with gingham flowers sewn on the knees—an obvious and unacceptable compromise.

The father said less and less about more and more. Whenever the subject of Charlotte came up he'd just say, Do whatever you want. Charlotte and her mother stopped going to Family Yoga and the father became angry saying he couldn't continue to go alone. It was Family Yoga and you needed to be a family to attend. "I'm sure you'll think of something," his wife said. He began sleeping in the guest bedroom and he used the guest bathroom as well. They all still did the same things—eating, watching television, sleeping, reading—but they did them at different times and in separate rooms.

It was the very short haircut that triggered the next confrontation. She had asked for a very short haircut and when her mother refused Charlotte cut it herself. She made such a mess of it that her mother was forced to take her to the beauty shop and have it fixed, and so she ended up with very short hair after all. On the way home, Charlotte and her mother stopped at the ice cream shop. Her mother left her alone at the table when she went to speak to Diane who was at the counter ordering something. When her mother came back to the table Charlotte had finished her strawberry swirl and saw that her mother's eyes were flooded. The Family Yoga teacher left quickly without saying hello or goodbye to Charlotte and she and her mother drove home listening to classical music and not speaking. Charlotte was asleep when her father got home that night so he didn't see her hair until the next morning.

    She sat at the breakfast table with him for a long time. He hadn't said anything about her hair. He would just look at her and then look away and not read his newspaper. Finally, he put down his coffee cup and said, "This will not stand."

He was angry but not shouting. He had a lot to say and didn't care if she was late for school. Charlotte didn't speak. She just let him talk and then, when he wasn't talking anymore, she realized that he was waiting. Waiting for her to respond.

"Say it. Say it, now, Charlotte."

She knew what he wanted her to say and she wished the words would come.

"Just say it, goddammit. Say it." He slapped his hand flat on the table making it hop ever so slightly. "Say it. Say 'I am a girl.'"

He had gone to her room and brought back a dress from her closet. It was lying on the chair between them like something dead or sleeping. Charlotte stood beside the chair as tall as she could make herself and felt her eyes grow watery and hot. Somehow, without her having raised her arms, he had managed to pull off her tee-shirt. Then, suddenly, between breaths practically, she found herself wearing the dress. He had slid it over her head. She couldn't even remember putting her arms into the sleeves, but nevertheless, there they were sticking out beneath silly little puffs of fabric. She still wore her jeans beneath the ruffles of the skirt and for that she was thankful.

Although Charlotte couldn't see her, she knew her mother had entered the room because she heard her say, "Stop it…please. Just stop it." But her father didn't hear or didn't care. His face was close to hers and she could feel his breath as he fastened the buttons on the front of the dress. There were six of them, each a different color and made to look like daisies. Her father was someone she no longer knew or trusted. She felt small and ridiculous in that dress. Sobs climbed up her throat and she wasn't sure what would happen next. He finished with the buttons and took hold of her shoulders, giving her a little shake.

"Say it." His voice was flat. "Say. It. Now."

She felt the word jump out of her mouth. "Girl." That was all she could manage. Then she said it once more, but it got caught in a gasp for air. She was crying without making a sound. Her father took a long hard breath and then he let go of her and looked away. They both felt victorious. Him, for what he made her say. Her, for what he couldn't make her feel.

In the night she heard them talking and crying. They were both crying. Her mother's voice was thin and cracked. She was telling the father what Charlotte already knew. That someone from Charlotte's school had called and told her that for three days now Charlotte has refused to speak. And she's refused to use either the girls' or the boys' restroom. Today she had been unable to hold her urine until she got home. It was terribly embarrassing for everyone in the class and her parents would have to come to the school first thing in morning.

As it turned out, Charlotte never went back to that school. The new school was further away and her father had to drive her there every morning. He no longer slept in the guest room. He slept with her mother again but her mother no longer got up to make Charlotte breakfast. Instead, her father would have milk and cereal on the table waiting for her. At the end of the day her mother would be waiting in the car to pick her up. Sometimes her mother would still be wearing her pajama top with a sweater over it or maybe still wearing her slippers instead of shoes. If she didn't have a headache she would let Charlotte play the radio.

The day of Show and Tell Charlotte wore a plaid skirt, a white blouse with lace on the collar and a green sweater. Her hair was long enough now to be pinned back with matching barrettes. She raised her hand when the teacher asked who wanted to be first. Charlotte stood in the center of the circle of small chairs surrounded by her classmates. She held a piece of notebook paper.

"What do you have there, Charlotte? Is it a story?"

"I wrote it last night," said Charlotte. In neat but crooked letters, down the left side of the page were the names of everyone she knew. Her mother and father, her grandparents, her cousins, favorite aunts and uncles, the kids she liked best at school and one special teacher. On the right side of the page she had made a list of everything she owned that she cared about. It started with her most precious possessions. A kite that she and her dad had made together and that they used to fly from an empty lot near their house; her bike with the customized handlebars; a pair of swim fins; a pair of skates; a canvas jacket with leather on the collar; all her books; all her CD's; the piece of green glass; a broken wristwatch. Finally, she had drawn lines from the possessions to the names of the people opposite. The lines crisscrossed over each other at steep angles creating a web between who she knew and what she had.

"What is it, Charlotte?" said the teacher again. "Aren't you going to read it to us?"

She gave the paper to the teacher and said, "May I use the restroom?"

"Yes, you may," said the teacher.

Charlotte walked out of the classroom and down the empty hall, then out of the school. The gate surrounding the playground wasn't locked and the crossing guard was talking to the bus driver and no one noticed her slip out. She began walking home. She wasn't certain she knew the way, but she wanted to try.

Shell Game with Organs

JACOB M. APPEL

Houdini urges me to disappear again. That's his panacea, his sovereign remedy. If he had his way, I'd vanish into thin air one night without a trace. On Lois, on mother, on him. And I suppose that would suit the old fellow just fine, too. The building crew would sniff him out eventually—find him belly-up on the carpet, caked in his own excrement, his kingdom lost for want of a saltine. Even then he'd be croaking "Disappear" through parched lips, I imagine, peddling spontaneous combustion to the Puerto Rican doorman and the one-armed super.

Houdini squeezes shut his onyx eyes, raises his wings to his cheeks. His voice is urgent. "Disappear! Disappear!"

"Shut up!"

Three hours straight I've debated alternatives, judged and unjudged myself. I don't *have* to visit mother. I don't *have* to play the shell game with organs. After tonight's show I could stow my equipment in the back of the truck and relocate to New York. Or rural Mauritania. A magician pulling off a disappearing act. Nothing could be more natural.

"How would you feel about rural Mauritania?" I ask Houdini. "The Sahara? The Casbah?"

Already I despise myself for shouting at him and I feed him a chocolate-coated wafer. He clasps the treat in his beak, slides it down his gullet with a tilt of his head. At least I can please someone, I think. So what if the snacks cause parrot cancer.

"What do you say we ditch mother and Lois and head off to Africa—just the two of us?"

"Disappear," Houdini retorts ambiguously, "Disappear." His vocabulary—the product of a magic routine we once did together—is frozen in time like a dead language.

Lois interrupts our conversation, struts in through the open door. Her heels pummel the hardwood in the foyer. We've been dating for almost a month now—which at forty-one means we're serious, that we know each other well—and still her vigor astounds me afresh at every meeting. She's so put-together, so fast-paced. She bounces through life like a wired kangaroo. If you saw her behind the counter at the crafts shop, you'd think she had kidneys.

"Ready to roll?" asks Lois. She plucks the lit cigarette from my mouth, tamps it out in the ceramic ashtray. The ashtray was stolen on a dare, appropriated from a chic downtown restaurant. I slid it into my sleeve on our first date.

"I was smoking that," I say. "Stocking up on nicotine for the hospital."

"Have a wafer," suggests Lois, popping the parrot treats like pills. "You shouldn't go to a hospital smelling like smoke."

I shouldn't go to a hospital at all, I want to answer. I shouldn't have to listen to a grown woman bleat senseless strings of gibberish.

"Mother smoked," I argue indifferently. "She won't care."

"And look what happened to her," says Lois. "Now let's get a move on. I hate being late."

"Disappear!" chimes in Houdini. "Disappear!"

I toss him another wafer, then cover his cage with an aquamarine bath towel.

We don't discuss the organ shell game on the way to Mass General. It's like a marriage proposal; it demands a yes or a no. Yet with every glance at Lois—with each glimpse of her bare thighs splayed on the passenger seat—I can't help reliving last night's afterglow, can't suppress the feel of her soft hands curling my pubic hair and playing across my flanks.

"Your kidneys," she cooed, sliding her fingers between the bed sheets and the small of my back. "I can feel them."

"Do they feel good?" I instantly second-guessed my own question: The same guilt I once felt when I waved to the one-armed super.

"I wish I could borrow one," said Lois.

"I wish you could too."

The words reached my brain seconds after they left my lips. Before I could decide whether I meant them—abstractly, of course—Lois bombarded me with this "emotional donor" business. She revealed that, thanks to the wonders of modern medicine, anyone who shares a blood type can share a kidney: Emotion is now thicker than blood.

"Body magic," she called it. "A shell game with organs." Three nights in the hospital and I'd have her off dialysis for life. Not to mention which, she added, the second kidney wasn't doing me any good where it was.

Lois made it sound as though she'd be doing me a favor: Relieving weight from my abdomen, giving my liver room to grow. She could have been a "Let's Make a Deal" contestant selecting Kidney #2. No emotional blackmail, no hang-dog looks. And that's probably why I like her. She's the only woman I've ever met who could compare invasive surgery to a sleight-of-hand.

"You ready for the show tonight?"

"Mother still wants me to kill her."

We're plodding through Mass Pike traffic, inching between Saturday afternoon's city-bound tide. Through the rear-view mirror I can spy into other vehicles: Here's an elderly couple bickering under matching sun-visors, there's three generations of a dark-skinned family sandwiched together like coldcuts. How easy their lives look through shatterproof glass. I have seen them from the stage, admired their simple wonder. Yet tonight I fear I will view them only as kidney packaging and potential matricides.

"Did you hear me?" I ask Lois. "She keeps making that sign with her hands. Like she's trying to silence a stranger or slaughter a chicken."

"You don't know what she means by it," says Lois.

"She's my mother," I say irritably. "I can tell. How am I supposed to concentrate tonight with all this to think about—with mother slicing her throat with her finger?"

Lois doesn't add, "And with your girlfriend begging for an organ handout." Most women would do that. At least most of the women I've dated. Instead, Lois says, "That's your problem. You're the magician."

So we drive in silence, sensing that last night has changed us: She has broached the kidney question and now it hangs over our relationship like some kind of love test.

I feel the need to argue my case again: That the magician's life does not easily permit this sort of commitment. Implicit for me, if not for her, is that the kidney and commitment questions are bound together like the sleeves of a straight jacket. I have loved other women. At seventeen I would have traded a lung for a blow job, but at forty-one a kidney for love seems like a risky venture. After all, I have only one spare kidney to give.

"I want you to speak with Dr. Sandkirk," says Lois. We're in the pay parking garage at the hospital; each minute of protest will add to the meter.

"Dr. Sandkirk," is all I answer.

"Yes, Dr. Sandkirk. The nephrologist."

Then we part ways, the echo of Lois's steps reverberating against the concrete. Her dialysis treatments permit me four hours alone with my mother.

Mother greets me from bed with a salvo of, "Late trees under water and each one has *his* own." That's the retired English teacher poking through, her speech without content yet impeccably grammatical. It's hard to imagine that a month ago, before the stroke, she was organizing Grey Panthers for a library boycott.

"Hi, Mom," I say, dropping a dry kiss on her leather cheek. "Bet you didn't think I was coming. "

"Late, late trees under water and each one has *his* own," she retorts. Her voice is weary, reproving. Her face looks fractured down the center and glued back together like a broken vase. When she speaks, the words bend around the corner of her mouth. She frowns at me and adds, emphatically, "Or *her* own."

I intend to tell her about the victory in the library strike, about the thousands of large print books that Boston Public has purchased under pressure. Instead, I find myself ready to shake her like an appliance on the blink. What right does she have to speak gibberish, to abandon me just when I've returned home for good? All those years on the road turning face cards into flowers, all those late night phone calls from Peoria and Yazoo City—and when I finally have a Boston gig, a sold-out debut in less than eight hours, the one person I thought I could depend on mutters, "Pills stock knowing that nurse, yes, yes," as though it were a schoolgirl's secret in need of release.

"Lois wants my kidneys," I finally say. "Well not both of them," I explain. "Only one."

In response, my mother slides her index finger across her jugular vein and closes her eyes. Her tongue falls from her mouth, her head sinks into the hospital pillows. There is no mistaking her meaning.

"I can't do that, Mother," I answer as I take her small hand in my large one. "Do you understand me? You know I can't do that. I can't. Besides, you'll be out on the picket lines in no time."

Mother opens her eyes, examines me with the wonder of a child. The doctors say the words go in with as little sense as they come out. My mother will never picket the library again, much less read a book. She is seventy-six years old. If we are lucky, chirps the underage rehabilitation therapist, she'll be able to count to ten and recite the days of the week within a year.

"Lois wants one of my kidneys," I say again. I produce a photograph from my wallet, point at Lois and then at my stomach. "Do you understand, Mother? Kid-ney. " To emphasize my claim, I draw a lima bean in the air with my finger.

My mother examines the photograph carefully and frowns in confusion. She stuffs imaginary food into her mouth, shrugs her shoulders to convey a question, and then rocks a make-believe child in her arms. This is a rare breakthrough: I understand her. She wants to know whether Lois is obese or pregnant.

"Dammit, Mom," I say, "Don't do this."

I might as well threaten to punish her: "Do as you're told or your father will take off his belt." It is no use. I know the whole goddamn situation is untenable. Cruel, even. She has lost her vocabulary, her memories. And she has lived too hard, too earnestly, to squander her final years distinguishing Mondays from Wednesdays.

"I have to go now, Mom. I have a show tonight. My Boston debut. I'm going to escape from chains and a straight jacket in an underwater tank."

"Either nurse or trees," she retorts vehemently. "Neither nurse nor trees."

Somehow this means that she's angry I will not kill her. Angry she doesn't have the strength, the means, to do it herself.

My cheek is wet when I press it against hers. Then I draw back her hair, brush the purple-gray strands into place, plant my lips on her forehead.

"Hang in there," I say. "Hang in there, Mom."

My mother leans forward in her bed, reaches out toward me with ghost-walk arms. I retreat rapidly to the lobby, to the small alcove of vending machines and pay telephones. The wall clock reminds me that I still have three hours to kill, so I collapse into a vinyl chair, my mind blank, and absorb the soothing murmur of the electronic ice maker.

"Rip Van Winkle returns," says Lois, startling me from my slumber. "Your twenty years are up, Rip. Time to find out who's dead and who's alive."

"Five more minutes," I say, twisting onto my stomach. I can feel the wooden arms of the chair jabbing my side.

"I'm going to have to get the cold water," Lois threatens. "Dr. Sandkirk doesn't have all day."

I vaguely recall this name, Sandkirk, so I blink the world into focus and rub the purple snow from my eyes. I find myself looking up into the bland, rosy face of the middle-aged physician.

Sandkirk defies my expectations. He has small round eyes, matching small round glasses. His head slopes from a broad brow to a narrow, almost inverted chin. All in all, he resembles a giant radish. So this is the celebrated nephrologist! I'd antici-

pated a full, glowing figure in a giant kidney costume, a man not
unlike the human peach in the Fruit of the Loom underwear
commercials.

"Dr. Sandkirk," Lois introduces us. "My boyfriend, Bill Sternberg, a.k.a. The Sleepy Santini. "

I grumble, "The Splendid Santini," as I shake his hand.

We follow Sandkirk along a maze of corridors, pass through a
series of fire proof doors. The doctor appears to know everybody.
He bestows his papal wave on emaciated old women stranded
in forgotten lounges and legless veterans who wheel together
in packs. All the while he shares his wisdom on the topics of
the day: The college selection process, the Red Sox's prospects
for the pennant. When we arrive at his office, we've somehow
jumped from the twelfth story to the fourteenth without switch-
ing floors. Medical magic. As yet, no mention of kidneys.

Sandkirk steers me to another vinyl chair. The office smells
mildly from mildew and damp paper. The nephrologist smells
pungently of aftershave lotion or raw bananas. His wall biogra-
phy tells me everything I need to know. He's a Princeton graduate, a champion Little League coach, a Fellow of the American
College of Physicians. All of this indicates a man with connec-
tions: One whose absence would be noted if I made him disappear.

Sandkirk says, "So, you're thinking about donating a kidney."

I answer, "That sounds like the title of a self-help book."

The doctor smiles; Lois crosses her legs.

"Thinking about it," I say. "Only thinking."

"That's good, Mr. Sternberg. I'd be the first to warn you
against a hasty decision. Because there *are* risks, you understand.
Of course, they're relatively minor risks. Yet they are risks. Like
driving a car or flying in an airplane. You don't think about the
risk every time you drive to work, but it exists nonetheless. Am

I making myself clear?"

"Risks are bad," I say. That's one of the few things I know for certain.

"And yet sometimes risks are necessary," says Sandkirk. I fear he will launch into a sermon on Alexander Fleming and the history of modern medicine. Instead, he outlines the advantages and drawbacks of the emotional donor. Lois listens attentively, glances at me periodically through the corners of her eyes. Sandirk narrates my recovery from post-op stitching to outpatient check-ups. After fifteen minutes, he has me feeling as though the entire procedure is as easy as a card trick. Nothing more than a shell game with organs. It's the non-givers, Sandkirk's "reluctant potentials," whose ignorance gives transplant a bad name. I feel guilty, as though I haven't signed the cornea release on the back of my driver's license.

"Of course I'll need some blood," the nephrologist concludes. "We need to confirm blood types and check for antibodies. Lois says you're both O-positives. Now roll up your sleeve."

He's rummaging through his filing cabinet for a needle when I stand up to excuse myself. "I'll think about it, Sandkirk," I offer. "But no blood. Not now. I have a show tonight."

"He does, doctor," Lois repeats apologetically.

"Oh," says Sandkirk. "Well good luck then. I'll see you soon."

We retreat into the corridor.

"What was that about'?" I demand as soon as we've escaped.

"What do you mean?"

"I mean that guy's knife-happy. I'm lucky he didn't do it right there on his desk with a scissors. "

Lois laughs. A short, sharp laugh. She asks, "So is that your answer?"

"I'm thinking," I say. "Still thinking."

"Well don't think too hard," she answers—and it's impossible to tell whether she's joking or sincere. "You might rupture your brain."

Then she kisses me on the lips, feels my crotch through my jeans. A nurse passes and throws me a "This is a hospital" look over a stack of hand-crocheted sweaters.

I kiss Lois harder and disappear into the warmth of her body. I suppress the urge to shout at the departed nurse, to tell her what she can do with her hospital. So what if it's a hospital! It's not a morgue. I'm ready to give the legless vets a thrill.

Lois pushes me back. "Down Big Boy," she says. "Time to go home."

I lean in for another kiss.

"Home," she says. "Later. You have a show tonight. Remember?"

"What show?"

"Magic," she answers.

I'm tired of doctors, tired of hospitals. I find myself wishing that mother would die and give Lois the kidney—and then I despise myself for the thought. That's not a solution. Not a realistic solution, at least. Vanishing, on the other hand, has a lot to be said for it. Almost too much to be said for it. Who'd miss me? I don't coach little league; I didn't go to Princeton. My alma mater, the exalted Garfield School of the Arts, went bust in the early 80's. The only two people who'd notice, who'd really notice, are Lois and mother—and with mother I don't know for certain. So there's only Lois. Lois. And, of course, Houdini. But Houdini's actively urging me to disappear.

"Disappear!" I call into the empty apartment. I pause at the kitchen table to sort through the afternoon's mail. "Isn't that right, Houdini? Disappear!"

But it's Houdini who's taken his own advice and gone belly-up on the floor of his cage. I stare at him in disbelief, but there is no disbelieving: Circles of blood ring his onyx eyes.

"Dammit!" I shout at him. "I warned you about those parrot treats. A thousand times I warned you. Just because you have a brain the size of a pea doesn't give you a right to have a parrot aneurysm on the night of my debut. Dammit!"

Twenty-five years I've had Houdini. Loved Houdini. Twenty-five years. He was my best friend, my brother.

"You stupid, stupid bird," I repeat as I cradle his lifeless body in my arms. I can still feel his warmth through the feathers. "Stupid, stupid bird."

I nuzzle his beak against my neck until his wings are slick with tears. "Stupid, stupid bird."

It's two hours later when I ring the one-armed super for a cardboard box. I wrap Houdini in his aquamarine towel and plant one final kiss on his tufted head. Good bye, old fellow. Good bye, old bird.

After phoning the theater to inform them that there's been a death in the family, I carry Houdini's coffin to the car. Then I drive out to Mass General, to be with my mother. Not to kill her, but to be with her. Tomorrow, I know, I must end things with Lois. But tonight, a middle-aged escape artist on the way to bury my closest friend, I feel the need to listen to my mother's gibberish. I want to hear her count Mondays and Wednesdays in the brief interval before she's gone.

Falling Off the George Washington Bridge

KERRY DOLAN

He had a father. The circle all began with him. Harried and stoop-shouldered, a chain smoker. He was a traveling salesman (he sold jars of apple sauce in ten different flavors) and slung a satchel across his shoulders, a black leather one packed with samples. He was not close to his father; his father's eyes never seemed able to bring any of them into focus, not his mother or the rest, gathered like ducklings around him, sickly ones who didn't get to eat much.

His father bought them a house, found on auction, a house built on landfill made of silt, sand, something. It made the floor sink in spots.

It was a town in New Jersey. Not Trenton, Passaic, Newark, or Camden. Not Paramus, Union, Teaneck, or Weehawken. Not even Hackensack, Elizabeth, or Jersey City. It was somewhere else.

He had a grandmother. She was supposed to visit for three months, from California, a state far away where he supposedly had some relatives though he'd never met any of them—California!!—but then she broke her hip, tumbling down the rickety stairs. Three months turned into eighteen years. Tommy had to give up his room, to give her a plump bed to lie on. That meant everyone else had to back up a space in the queue. She spent most of her time lying in that bed, like a queen.

No one liked the grandmother. She had illnesses, but not ones you could pinpoint. She talked to herself and shuffled around the hallway in the middle of the night, knocking into things. She was almost completely deaf so she didn't realize the ruckus she was making, must have thought she was just dropping feathers in her wake. At dinner, she would send his mother's pork chops back, the ones she had cooked hastily, to a crisp leather. Or else she would sit at the table with a scowl on her face while the rest of them were trying to eat.

It was just another ingredient to add to the mix.

He had a stairway. It was crooked and twisty with steps only as thick as dwarves' feet. It made the daily journey up and down to the bedrooms a life-imperilling task. "We have to get new stairs," his father would say. He'd been saying that for as long as Timmy could remember, for at least eighteen years. On the way up the stairway, he'd run into the others. They were boys most of them, with names ending in -ee. Tommy, Terry, Billy, Bobby, Petey, Mikey. There were some girls thrown in, too. They might as well be numbers, crumpled tickets you got on line at the bakery. He was Number Six. That's how he thought of it.

He had a bathroom. It was his favorite room in the house, though he didn't get to spend much time in there. Still, he'd memorized each spot, each check on the floor, each squashed spider or waterbug that his brothers, all lazy, had forgotten to clean. In his mind he made the spot larger than it was. In the

bathroom he could spend time at his favorite activities: He liked
sitting on the toilet, long past doing his business, with the rustle
of the newspaper; or rubbing himself to the ticking of the over-
head electric light bulb. He liked sitting in the bath even after
the water was cold. He liked to think, and though his mind was
often blank—what was there to think about?—to him, this was
freedom.

He had a priest. Father Maloney. Maloney had taken him aside
once and told him he had some special skills as an altar boy, that
he handled the communion plate with deftness and grace. Father M. told him that he might want to take those skills further,
to another level. He thought, briefly, about becoming a priest. It
gave him a burning, a happy one, deep in the pit of his stomach.
Before this, there was nothing he'd been particularly good at. In
the mornings, he'd never been an eager riser; no motive to lift his
head from the pillow. He wondered if he'd ever had that motive;
probably back when he was a little kid, but of course he couldn't
remember all the way back then. In pictures, in childhood, he'd
smiled a lot, even laughed. He couldn't remember what he'd
laughed about; what would he have found funny? So for awhile,
the priest thing gave him a lantern in the distance. It gave him a
track where none existed. But then he thought: all those priests
crowded together, waiting to use the bathroom.

He had girlfriends. He remembered ankle bracelets, flannel
shirts, tits that looked sad, vulnerable, as they poured out, the
white, pure white of the Irish ones, and the large brown-nippled
Italian girls' that looked always, in his mind, more slutty, yet
exciting; like the cheap kind of bandaids. He remembered them
saying, whimpering like stepped-on cats, Be gentle, okay?, as

they rustled in the bony ice-cold backseat of the car, first Tommy's, then Billy's, two more numbers, then his. He'd always arrived too late.

There were some pets, sure. That was a bright spot. Dogs mostly, though they all seemed to die untimely deaths. One run over by a UPS truck, one nicked in the head by a snow plow, one, a collie that bred tumors, oozers they had to cover with masking tape and cotton balls. It seemed they had a new dog every year and just by the time they named the thing, it up and croaked. His favorite, Edgar, was the one that got away, last seen trotting off in the direction of Pennsylvania.

He thought about leaving, sometimes, like Edgar. But he couldn't really imagine it, except in some far off place in the back of his head, a little spot whose view was blocked most of the time. His legs were caught in sludge.

With the nine of them there were weddings, kids, divorces. They came and went out of the house. You couldn't chart the progress in the usual sense: their lives were circles instead of lines. Apple sauce, landfill, nothing solid.

Kathy, one girlfriend, stuck around for a while. Kathy and Timmy. Timmy and Kathy. She talked of weddings. It went on for—what?—three years. She corralled him into everything. She wanted to be a nurse's assistant, had clean white teeth, freckled arms, a gold cross. She buzzed around him like an irritant. He hated that gold against freckles. He didn't do anything to keep her and she kept coming back. He found a distinct pleasure in meanness, in refusing to say I love you. He couldn't help it, seeing how far he could push it.

It seemed the more he shrugged them off the more they stuck

to him. They were barnacles. They were starfish, with clinging tentacles.

Sheryl wasn't like that. Sheryl was like climbing a slippery slope without wallet or car keys. She wasn't good for him, his mother said, not like that Kathy was. He knew that.

He felt something for his mother. Whenever he ran into her in the kitchen late at night after he got off from the cargo shift, standing there in her sickly brown robe, warming a dented pot of milk, something flickered inside him, like a staticky radio. He remembered childhood and wet sweaters in snow, leftover meatball sandwiches and hot chocolate. She looked older now, her hair strewn gray. She was alone, in a house full of children and husbands and mother-in-laws. He tried to avoid these meetings.

He had a boss. Well, bosses. He'd had lots of jobs, some for a few months, in varying degrees of worseness. He punched time clocks, usually a few minutes late. There were a few variations in the jobs: sometimes he made friends, sometimes he didn't; sometimes the coffee room had donuts, glazed ones melted like snot, sometimes it didn't; sometimes the time clock was by the door, sometimes it was near the coffee room; sometimes they gave you ear plugs, or a mouth mask, plastic eye goggles, sometimes they didn't.

His longest stint was as a cargo handler at Newark Airport. At least it was union.

It was better than the previous job he'd had at the Oreo factory—well, not Oreo, but a competing brand. In the coffee room his boss kept a plate of cookies, cracked ones, or laced with gunk, for a special treat.

The best gig he'd had—easy money—was cleaning asbestos:

eighteen dollars an hour. He'd made friends at that one. His friends would joke: look my hands are burning off! My nose! I'm blind! My lungs are black! That was a good job.

It was an accident. He'd slipped on the ice. They'd climbed the rink after hours. He was drunk, shitfaced. One of the girlfriends, Sheryl, was there, but she was shitfaced too. He didn't know, couldn't remember, whose idea it was, to climb the rink, hop the fence for a moment of wildness. He remembered Sheryl laughing, a hearty mannish chuckle as he hit the surface. She wore a nubbly green scarf too big for her, triple wound around her neck, and a light blue ski jacket from Goodwill. Roots in her hair, a cigarette. Why was she laughing? He felt no sound as he was falling, the world curiously still, clear. He could see it all, the leaving, the coming. He was alone. He'd always been alone.

Maybe things could have gone differently. If Sheryl hadn't kept dropping all of those dimes out of her pocket. If she'd remembered the number for 911. If the pay phones outside the rink hadn't been busted. If she hadn't had to walk a mile and a half along the highway to the Seven-11. She flagged down cars. She'd tried. That's what she told people. She was screaming. She thought she was screaming. Like a dream of a tidal wave or being naked—wasn't she screaming?

Instead she just drove him, jittery and key-dropping, back to her apartment and fell asleep. That was the problem.

For years, he'd had tics, nervous ones. Sniffing, coughing, eye-blinking. Palm-scratching. It started when he was in Catholic school, when he knew he could get his head banged against the blackboard if he made one false move. That's what happened to

Joey Murphy when he coughed too much. He couldn't help it. Knowing he couldn't make a gesture made him do it; it made him itching to do it even more. So he'd had lots of knocks on the head: rulers, belts, erasers, chalkboards, desks. He used to think his head was invincible. He used to think his head was as hard as a helmet on a Viking. He used to think God—this is when he most believed in him—had given him one little thing to be proud of.

Afterwards he couldn't remember as much. But what he did wasn't good. Now the nine really mushed together. They gathered around his bed. They'd moved his grandmother into the attic. He'd gotten the bed, finally.

Sheryl came for awhile then left. She disappeared. He didn't blame her really. Now all he had was the nine of them huddled around. Now things drifted in and out like signals on a short wave radio.

Kathy—she would've stuck around. He was missing her now, a little.

Number Two was back with a few kids in tow, loud and empty of cuteness. Number Five, Number Eight and Number Nine— they'd never left. Number Four had escaped but she'd be back soon. Number One—he had a house down the street and always came over, especially when he heard a rumor concerning chicken pot pie. Number Three and his wife were out of work—so they got the cot in the basement. Oh and the grandmother. His father ranted and raved: the house was sinking lazy good for nothings did they think he was a millionaire did they forget what it meant to earn an honest buck now he'd really have to fix the stairs what with all the extra feet but why should he have to pay for it with all his hard-earned money.

None of the numbers paid much attention to him.

He had a confessional. During his altar boy days he'd sneak in, not to confess—he didn't believe in that, or not mainly—but just to sit. He'd sneak in long after the priests' listening hours were over, before he left for home, walked the two miles for dinner, for winter meatloaf or pot roast. It was a small box but he didn't feel crowded: he felt surrounded, in fullness, complete. He liked the quiet. He liked the velvet, the fall of the curtains, the sound—the soundlessness—of the sacred. Sometimes he closed his eyes, listening.

He had a bed, a bedroom, now. After awhile, he got out of the bed but he had trouble keeping a job. He was drinking a lot, wasn't the same, couldn't get his mind fixed on the proper equations. The cargo stint—that was long gone. His father was around more—the apple sauce field was drying up—he was home like a chafing rash. His father had to take account of him now. They fought. He, Number Six, drank and forgot things and had fits and everyone finally was a little afraid of him. I'm gonna have to throw you out his father would say. They noticed him, all right. They noticed him.

It was good while it lasted. Eventually the grandmother needed the bed back. She complained it was cold up in the attic. She complained she needed the bed for her sciatica and neuralgia and, also, her recently developed migraines. Perhaps it was all the yelling in the house, she said. Plus her hip again, it was broken for the fifth time, though his mother swore she did it on purpose, just hurled herself down the stairs for a bit of attention.

Fortunately, there was still the couch with the pull-out sofa. He liked to stay up late into the night, covered with a thin yellow blanket, radio tuned dimly to the oldies station.

He remembered, kept remembering, that fall towards ice: as the world held its place, he was outside it, just floating, weightless, like an astronaut, or a meteor. He was outside it all. It would be like that with the bridge too. The rush towards water, the possibilities. The brief traversal of silence. You see, that's what people didn't get: the point of the jump was the jump.

Gorgeous World

ALICIA GIFFORD

I've forgiven my mother; she didn't know what she was doing. She heard voices, had visions. She imagined herself to be a
prophet named Helen when her real name was Marge. When she
learned she was pregnant with me she scored some Thalidomide
from my grandparents' Nicaraguan housekeeper whose mother
got it on the black market to treat her skin leprosy. I know the
whole story. My mother wanted a "special" baby. She thought
it would be good for Helen the Prophet to have a humanity
challenge, something grotesque. She chowed Thalidomide down
through her first trimester.

I was born in 1970 in Burbank, California with flipper arms,
mini legs and normal-sized feet. My overall look is just like a
penguin. I'm deaf in my right ear and I've had five operations to
fix up a cleft palate so sometimes I honk. My lower jaw didn't
develop right, like a character on *The Simpsons*.

"*Perfect*," my mother said about me.

If I look in the mirror just right I see how I might've looked
if my mother hadn't messed with Thalidomide. I might've been
good looking. Mainly though, I don't look in mirrors.

My name is Robert but I go by "Penguin" and I work as a

penguin at the Home Show. I'm a trademark-mascot for Ames Igloos—tents you inflate with a built-in inflator so they're insulated; and then you can A/C them with a self-contained coolant system, or heat them with a built in heater. It looks just like an igloo with all the comforts. Buzz Ames invented them and he's getting rich too. Every urban cowboy with an SUV and a backpack has to have an Ames Igloo.

My job at the Home Show is to waddle back and forth on a platform dressed in a custom-made penguin outfit and orange webbed feet. I draw people like shit draws flies. They watch me in my cozy Igloo, relaxed and smoking a fat cigar attached by a device to my flipper since the orange webbed feet keep me from using my feet to smoke. I honk for the crowd and get applause. I'm with Buzz Ames seven years now, since I was twenty, and we get along fine. We travel towing Buzz's Airstream—the Land Yacht—and I like it. I've been to forty-eight states and Buzz wants to hit Alaska soon. I sleep in an Ames Igloo in the trailer park where Buzz hitches up his trailer—always pitching product. They're comfortable. Total quality.

Buzz likes women, has a new one every night, if he wants. He'll yak on his cell phone with his wife and kids in San Diego, a naked woman curled around him.

"Don't you feel guilty?" I ask.

"Naw," he says. "Just a piece of ass." He's about as close to family as I've got.

My mother and I lived with my grandparents. We never knew my father. I didn't know my mother was crazy. I thought she was beautiful.

On my sixth birthday my mother and I stole Gram's car— Helen the Prophetess wasn't supposed to drive. We got hot dogs, ice cream, stuff she usually wouldn't let me eat. We went to the pet store and looked at puppies and kittens, fish, turtles, smelled the pet store smells. We drove to Von's, parked in the lot, and then walked onto the Pass Avenue overpass of the 134 Freeway.

She climbed on the guardrail in her white prophet dress, her long, red hair blowing out behind. She looked to the heavens, spread her arms wide and flew in a dead drop down to the freeway where she was hit by about a dozen cars in a minute. *Take me! Take me!* I shrieked, scuttling back and forth, my flippers bloodied from scraping them on the metal guardrail, trying to join her.

I had problems after that. I realized I was a freak and I refused to leave the house. My grandparents were teachers, Granddaddy taught philosophy at a community college and my Grams taught high school English. They home schooled me and I got a better education from them than I ever would've in school.

Granddaddy was an atheist. "Life's meaningless," he said. "We push a rock up a hill, it rolls down; we push it up again. Then we die. It's that absurd. Your only hope is to enjoy the pushing."

"Don't listen to him," Grams said. "He doesn't believe a word of it." She made me read books, from classics to pulp fiction. I couldn't get enough, Grams supplying me from the library. I could lose myself there, movies too. We watched movies everyday.

When I was eighteen I was as self sufficient as someone like me can be. Gram's arthritis became torture for her and her heart was bad. She was losing her sight and Granddaddy was losing his mind, and he knew it. They didn't want to squander their assets on institutions. They didn't want to be without one another. "We're done," they said.

They told me that they were leaving me everything, and that financially, I'd be okay for a while, until I figured out a way to earn a living. Grams gave me a comprehensive reading list. "These books will enrich your life," she said, "and give you this gorgeous world."

"Life's a crapshoot," Granddaddy said. "Load the dice anyway you can." He grabbed me. "Sorry about your mother," he said into my hair. I kissed him, my Grams, told them how much I loved them, how grateful I was. We cried, couldn't help it. Then they went to the garage that they'd sealed with wet towels, the Oldsmobile already running. They told me to call the police after an hour, and that's what I did.

The house they left me in Burbank I rent to a pair of twin sisters, so I have some income there. When I'm in town I stay there, in my old basement apartment. I'm happy like this, I don't think about loneliness anyway, and then Ray Ann Karnowski comes into my life.

Ray Ann is a blonde-haired, blue-eyed dwarf girl that I met doing the Home Show in Orange County, California. First I see her hanging around, staring, nothing I'm not used to. She comes every day for a week in a different colored tube top, the same faded denim mini skirt, and red cowboy boots. She's got big spirals of yellow hair and a heavy hand with make-up. On our last day I ask her if she'd like to join me for a smoke.

"Yeth," she says. I remove the webbed feet, slip on sandals and we walk outside the Convention Center. We heave our bodies up onto a bench and I light her a Lucky Strike using my feet. I hand it to her and she pats my leg with a hand that looks like the paw of a Saint Bernard. We smoke in silence for a while, ignoring the stares of all the good folk visiting the Home Show.

She gives me a sidelong look through blue-hooded eyes caked thick with black. She's familiar to me and then it hits me: she looks just like Miss Piggy.

"I like penguins," she says. She lisps all her S's.

"I like pigs," I say. I've got a trigger retort reflex and I see I hurt her feelings. "I mean I *really* like pigs. Smarter'n dogs. Smarter than penguins, for sure."

"I'm sensitive because sometimes people call me Miss Piggy," she says.

"Really," I say.

"What's your story anyway?" she asks. She swings her chunky, short legs, takes a long drag off the cigarette and blows perfect, concentric O's from dark, magenta lips. I give her my standard bio about Thalidomide, leaving out the insane mother part.

"I'm a Little Person, duh," she says. "Do you have a penis?"

My package is normal. I'm tortured by horniness and you can imagine it's not easy for a guy like me to get laid. I'm a virgin. I can masturbate with my feet but it's exhausting. I tried devices that came in plain brown wrappers from the Internet—artificial vaginas, blow-up dolls, blow-up *child* dolls—sleazy stuff. The best thing was the worst thing: a medium-rare rump roast. I told myself the whole time it was in the oven that it was just dinner but I *knew* I was going to fuck it. Trying not to think about what I was doing, I cut a hole in it, buttered it and then I fucked it in the kitchen with the lights off while it was still warm, pretend-ing with all my might it was Natalie Portman. What I wouldn't give for some genuine female anatomy. What I wouldn't give for a girlfriend.

"Nothing wrong with me there," I say, flapping my flippers for emphasis. I take a long drag and pull my lips back hard, trying to make a tough guy face, hissing out my smoke. I'm still in the penguin costume.

"I have epilepsy," she says. "Grand Ma seizures." She shrugs her thick little pork shoulders. "Luck of the Irish I guess."

"You Irish?"

"Polish," she says. "It's just an expression, duh. I'm Ray Ann. Ray Ann Karnowski."

"I'm Penguin," I say.

"There's something about you." She narrows her eyes and blows smoke out the side of her mouth. "You got a place?"

"Yeah I got a place." We're staying at a swell trailer park just out of Irvine. She leans back on the bench and throws back her head. I can see her nipples poking through her orange tube top like the ends of lemons.

"Let me see if my boss'll let me off early," I say.

When I go in to talk to Buzz about leaving, he grins. "Not unless you got a hot date." I grin back and his face marvels. "No shit? Get *out* of here." He claps me on the back.

Ray Ann's got a black '67 Mustang outfitted for midgets. We get into it and head to Irvine. I've figured if I ever were to get laid it'd be with someone along the lines of Ray Ann. I hope I like her. I'm nervous and hard as a block of ice the whole way to the Igloo.

Ray Ann sings to a "Best of the Carpenters" tape. *Rainy day-sth and Mondaysth al-waysth get me*—she puts her paw on her heart—*do-o-wn*. "I was so sad when she died," she says wistfully. "Karen Carpenter was the finest singer of the century."

I hate the Carpenters. "She's great," I say.

We're wailing on *We've Only Just Begun* when we reach the Sunny Daze Trailer Resort. We park and get out of the car.

"Ooooh, nice trailer," she says. "A beauty."

"That's my place, out back," I say. She looks at the Igloo.

"Darling," she coos. "Even better."

I tell her to go ahead and get into the Igloo while I change out of my penguin garb in the trailer.

"Don't be too long," she says, ducking inside.

I change my clothes and do a quick freshen up at the sink. I take deep breaths. I help myself to a couple of Buzz's Trojans.

This is it, I tell myself.

I enter the Igloo with a couple of cold Rolling Rock long-necks clutched to my chest.

"Groovy," she says. "I LOVE beer."

She's lying down, propped up on her elbow, boots off. She takes a long pull off the beer. "Ahhh," she says.

I sit and gulp down beer using my feet.

"That's amazing, how you use your feet like that," she says.

"Yeah, well." Surgeons wanted to operate on my flippers and fit me with artificial arms but my grandparents said no and I'm glad. I've heard of other thalidomiders who've done it only to chuck the prostheses because they hated them, ending up with nothing. I can type, strum a guitar, smoke, do just about anything with my feet that hands can do. My flippers are useful, too. They're short but I have an elbow joint and then the forearm part tapers into a paddle I can curl. I can carry things, clutched to my chest. My legs are sturdy and normal but the bone shafts didn't grow so they're short. I get around just fine on them.

Ray Ann chugs down that beer in no time. I go back to the trailer and bring out two more and she guzzles both of them while I work on the first one.

"*Bwaaaaaaaap!*"

"Nice burp," I say.

" 'xcusthe," she says. She reaches for me then, pulls me down and rolls on top of me. She presses her lips on mine and thrusts her fat tongue down my throat. I like it.

We grope, wrestle; she's got her clothes off and her two white tits and cherry nipples look like a twin ice cream sundaes. She's shaved her pussy and when I catch a glimpse of the glistening pink I nearly come.

"Gnash the gash, baby," she says in a growly voice. "I'm opened wide for chunky."

Ray Ann's soft, musky flesh pressed to me is unimaginable. Maybe there is a God. She straddles me, bounces—her big round tits brush my face, my tongue. I come—a burst straight out her spine that circles the earth—the Penguin Meteor. I see God. Feel Him. I get why people think He exists, anyway. Then I snuffle like a baby.

Ray Ann cradles my head. "Jeez, are you *crying*?" She kisses my wet cheeks. "You are *hot*, baby." She licks her finger, puts it to her butt and makes a sizzling noise.

We smoke my last two cigarettes and then, she burrows into me, raising my flipper and tucking it behind her neck. In thirty seconds she's snoring on my chest. Saliva slides out the side of her mouth and runs down along my ribs to my sheet. She moves in closer, snugger, wrapping my legs with hers. She's so beautiful! I blink tears and float on the ceiling of the Igloo. I feel bliss. Connected. Like an ordinary Joe.

I can smell her on my upper lip and I relive the sex while she sleeps, making me hard again. Dusk falls. Buzz pulls up in his Jeep and parks next to Ray Ann's Mustang. *If this igloo's a-rockin', don't come a-knockin'* he sings. I honk a reply. Ray Ann lets a wet fart and I grin in the dark. I grin until I fall sleep, inhaling her vapors.

When I wake up, it's three in the morning. Ray Ann's bunched down around my feet with my penis in her mouth, working it like a leg of chicken. Soon I'm spurting down her throat.

"How was that Pengie?" she says breathing beer and cum in my face.

I make soft honking noises. "Heaven."

"We're going to have so much fun together," she says. "I can't wait to hit the road with you guys."

My scalp shrinks and some hairs stand on end. "We're taking time *off* the road. This is our last gig for two months," I say.

"So?"

"I go to Burbank and Buzz drives home to San Diego."

"I LOVE Burbank," she says. "Where do we stay?"

I sift through a flight of ideas. What the hell?

"We stay in a basement apartment in my house that I rent to some sisters."

"I LOVE basements," she says.

Luce and Lila bend and hug me. "So *good* to see you Robert," says one of them. They won't call me Penguin.

"You look *fine*," says the other.

The house smells great. "We got the smoker going. Ribs and a brisket," they say in unison.

I never know which one's Luce, which Lila. Their grizzled hair is processed and blown out in big, bouffant do's reminiscent of The Supremes in the early '60's. They're tall, slender and tilt sideways to their left when they stand or sit. They wear matching yellow gingham shirtwaist dresses that show off the milk chocolate of their skin, and nurse's shoes. They must be pushing seventy.

"I brought a friend this time," I say.

"Glory, come on, wonderful news. Where is he?" They look out the door in a synchronized motion.

"*She*'ll be right back. She went to get some cigarettes."

Luce and Lila look at each other with raised eyebrows.

"Land," they say together. "Well come in, your room's all ready."

Just then Ray Ann screeches into the driveway and we watch her jump out of her car and swagger over to us carrying two six-packs with two bottles missing.

"Nice place," she says looking around. She sees Lila and Luce. "Twins! *Sisters*. You're sisters—and you're—*sistahs*." She widens her eyes and grins like a maniac.

"Ray Ann—Lila and Luce," I say.

"Don't bother saying who's who. Y'all look alike to me." She looks at each of us with the same manic face. "It's a *joke*, DUH. Which way to our room?"

Lila invites us to have supper in about an hour and we agree. I take Ray Ann down in the little elevator to my basement apartment. The sisters have put sweet smelling roses from the garden in a vase.

"I think I'm going to like it here," Ray Ann says, running around, poking in the closet, the bathroom. She flops on the bed that sits directly on the painted concrete floor and rips open a beer, tilts her head back and chugs it.

"Is that an icicle in your pocket or are you just happy to see me," she says. She sets down the beer, opens her legs and runs her tongue around her lips. It works for me. Next thing we're thrashing in bed for a couple of hours, skipping dinner with Lila and Luce.

"Hand me—oops! *Foot* me a Kleenex, Sugar." I give her one and she mops up the mess between her legs. We didn't use a condom. I couldn't get it on by myself and she refused. "What's the worst that can happen?" she says. "Let go, let God."

She talks about her messed up female parts askew in her interior, tangled tubes, crusted ovaries. She talks about operations she's had, teeth that were pulled, her battle with constipation. She says everything happens for a reason and it's our karma to be together now. She thinks she knows me from a previous life, that we could be soul mates. If I'd heard all this last week I might've called it drivel but now my mind's wide-open.

Her father, a dead dwarf actor, provided the trust fund she lives on. She'd been living with her mother and sister, both normal sized and they don't get along. "Try growing up with a fucking prom queen," she said about her younger sister. "I'm like the evil pet chimpanzee there. My mother's always bitching. Says I embarrass her; that I drink too much. She wants to put me in rehab. Fuck her."

Over the next few weeks Luce and Lila watch with arms folded and leaning like two trees blown by the same wind as Ray

Ann staggers around like she's aboard rough seas.

"She's fun loving," they say with tight lips as Ray Ann knocks back four shots of tequila and shimmies to Barry Manilow's *Copa Cabana.*

The straight fact is that Ray Ann is loud and sloppy drunk almost every day. I'm not sure she's ever read a book. But she *is* fun loving. And one hundred percent woman. Lying next to her, hearing her gentle snores, watching her wet, slack mouth move like she's praying, I get it. I get the sappy songs. I get Romeo and Juliet. I get why every other movie and novel is about love.

"Do you like drugs?" she asks.

"Never done any."

"I used to do drugs," she says. "I like them, duh, but I get more seizures." She shrugs.

"How'd you get a driver's license, anyway," I ask.

"Driver's license?" she says.

She asks me if I got teased much, growing up. I tell her I rarely left the house, except to get surgeries or speech therapy.

"You're lucky," she says. "I went to Beverly Hills High and had zits galore. This one girl said I grew maggots in my face. She and her friends made fun of me for years." She smiles with watery eyes and lights a new cigarette with the butt of the old one. "I fucked their boyfriends to get my self esteem back. *They* didn't think I had maggots." She takes my face in her two hands. "You're sweet. Respectful. You make me feel good about myself, beautiful. And look at all these books—you're smart, like a fuck- ing *genius.*" She hugs me and I could bust like a piñata, pour out hearts and flowers.

Ray Ann takes me clothes shopping at Snow White's Den, a shop for dwarves or "Little People" as she insists on saying. In a toy store I get big, pink, rubber hands and I wave to everyone as we strut down the Venice boardwalk, tasting the salt in the air, the ocean glittery with sun and us, giddy in spangled vests, satin shirts and cowboy hats, fitting right into the Venice freak show. It's *fun*.

We go to restaurants and for the first time, I eat in public, Ray Ann feeding me at first and then me using the silverware with my feet. "Take a picture, it'll last longer," Ray Ann says when people stare. We see movies and go to Disneyland. We screw like rodents. I engage with the absurd world outside the Home Show, and I like it.

One night after we'd been together for a month Ray Ann tells me she's going to visit her friend Graciela, have a hen session. We'd been inseparable until then. "Go ahead," I say, but I miss her soon as she leaves. Two o'clock in the morning, she's still not back. I watch TV, smoke up all my cigarettes. At four I walk down to the *7-Eleven* and buy some more. I fall asleep and then Ray Ann's waking me up a few hours later. She's sweaty, stinks, has dark circles under her eyes

"I had a seizure," she says. "Wiped me out. I slept at Graciela's."

"I wish you'd called. Luce and Lila want us to have brunch."

She's agitated, shaky. She sits and then paces, lies down and springs up. She lights a cigarette when she's already got two going.

"We had a little toot," she says, licking her lips. "I need a drink." She pours herself a tall Southern Comfort and gulps it down. She pours herself another one, gets half way through it and then falls asleep with the glass in her hand.

Once she's settled I go by myself to eat with Luce and Lila.

"Ray Ann under weather?" they ask.

"She had a seizure—wipes her out."

"Drinking's no good for that," one says, the other nodding in agreement. "Girl's got a bottle problem, Robert, looking to be *your* problem."

"I don't remember asking for opinions," I say, thinking how I'd never seen what nosy biddies these two really are. "Excuse me, I've lost my appetite."

I go downstairs and munch on three-day-old pizza while Ray Ann snores.

A few days later Ray Ann tells me we're invited to a party given by her friends. "These people are like *family* to me," she says, "and they can't wait to meet you." I have a jinxed feeling about it, but she's excited and insistent and hey, it might be nice to have friends.

We show up at the party in a bungalow style home in Highland Park, mainly biker types and hard looking women. Kegs of beer sit on a wood table in the middle of the room. Everyone stares at us but Ray Ann's oblivious.

"Pengie," she says with her wide-eyed manic face, "you just gotta try crank—you'll *love* it."

"I don't—"

"C'mon." She pulls me to where a couple of people are bent over a table, chopping chunks into powder.

A burly guy with long, greasy hair, a leather vest and no shirt looks at her. "Well if it ain't Miss Piggy," he says. He looks at me. "And Kermit."

I laugh way too loud. Ray Ann's only got eyes for the meth. "C'mon Toto. Fix us up."

Toto stares at me. "Jesus Christ," he mutters, "she looks fucking *normal* next to you." Someone puts a straw and a plate of methamphetamine to Ray Ann's nose and she snorts it up, wagging her rear like a puppy.

"Ever seen a penguin on speed?" she says in a high-pitched titter. "Your turn Pengie."

"Sure," I say, "but first, where's the bathroom?"

Toto points to a hallway. "Follow the yellow brick road," he says. Ray Ann throws her head back with her mouth wide open and squeals.

In the bathroom I lean my forehead on the cold sink. I hate this party. I don't want to speed or trip or drink myself stupid. These people are fucking *scary*. I want to get Ray Ann out of here. I want her to have different friends. I want her to drink less, to not do drugs.

I want her to be someone else. I take this in and get a sinking feeling worse than loneliness. I try to rev up the love, the excitement, but I just want to go home.

I go back out to beg her to leave but they're gone. I wander around, ignoring the stares, trying not to be scared. I end up back at the bathroom. The door's open so I step inside to hide and think—and there's Toto on the toilet, smoking a cigarette and Ray Ann's in front of him, blowing him like a porno video in fast-forward. He sees me and puts his head back, exhales a stream of smoke and closes his eyes. I swallow a mini-vomit and spin around to leave but then he lets out an unearthly screech and I turn back to see Ray Ann in a seizure on the floor with blood spurting from her mouth. She goes rigid and then flops like a landed halibut. Blood gushes from a meaty hole where Toto's penis used to be; his penis that's now clenched between her small, gory teeth, pink foam pouring out on either side; and then it disappears like she's swallowed it. She bucks and flops on the floor turning purple while Toto goes pearl-eyed, twists off the toilet in a slow slide and his big head hits the tile floor with a hollow thunk. *It's that absurd*, my Granddaddy whispers in my ear.

I stick my head out the door and honk with all I've got.

A Heimlich maneuver might've saved her but with her convulsing like that and Toto's situation flooding the bathroom floor with blood, no one thought of it. By the time the paramedics figured it out they couldn't revive her. The convulsions burned up her oxygen, they said.

They removed the penis from her airway, packed it in ice to sew it back on but from what I saw they'd have as much luck sewing on ground round.

I'm waiting with her body for the coroner and man she looks awful: big head torqued all crazy, yellow hair soaked in blood; face steel-colored and staring; her whole existence reduced to something as perishable as pork. Poor Ray Ann. I feel grief like I feel grief for all lonely, fucked-up people. Lonely and fucked-up is what we had in common. Now I don't have to figure out if that's enough.

The coroner tags, bags and takes her away, and then a cop drives me home after I give my statement and tell him what I know about her next of kin. "You take care of yourself," he says, avoiding my eyes.

In my room I kick an empty bottle of Southern Comfort and it clinks into some beer bottles, toppling them like bowling pins. I've never felt so alone. I tell myself that maybe something good *can* happen some day. It almost happened—it *kind of* happened with Ray Ann—

I crawl into bed, and I'm so tired I can't keep from crying and then the strangled honking noises make me hate myself, and I can't wait to fall sleep.

❧ *Term* ❧

ALISON LEE KINNEY

Adam wrote in the baby's album, "Week 16, Day 110: We visited your midwife Carmen today. She says you're thriving! Next week, the amnio and our first ultrasound."

He loved Carmen's bright, orange-painted birthing center, with the Mary Cassatt prints and tanks of tropical fish. Hiring a nurse midwife had been his idea; he and Suzanne had known too many doctors and hospitals. But Suzanne had resisted the idea at first: "It sounds a little hippy-dippy to me." She always put more faith in routines, even hateful ones, than in the unknown. Yet even she couldn't fail to be impressed by Carmen's professionalism and pragmatism, and she began to relax, letting go of her resentments and fear. This was how childbirth should be, Adam felt, and it was time for them to do things the way they wanted to.

Today he had told Carmen, "We don't like the risks. We're sick of tests and treatments."

"I understand. I don't generally approve of invasive procedures either, but," Carmen had shrugged, "you've waited ten years for this pregnancy. You're both forty-one. I think you should err on the side of caution."

He clasped his wife's hand. "Suzanne and I already know we can raise a disabled child."

Carmen said, "It's not just your feelings about Down Syndrome you have to think about," and talked about finances, health care, and education.

Suzanne weighed in. "Carmen's right." And that was that.

While Suzanne was driving him back to work, he said, "When I was in grade school, the special kids would hang around us, trying to fit in, laughing at all the jokes we cracked at their expense. They didn't know how mean the jokes were. I hope. I'd hate for my kid to go through that."

Suzanne said, "You think that's bad? Then they wind up institutionalized, until the government shuts down the mental hospitals and makes them homeless. Then they go crazy and push somebody in front of a train and get the electric chair, without ever knowing what they've done."

"Or they end up president!"

She snorted. "And then what about the poor kid's sex life? How do you deal with that?"

He reached over to smooth the crease between her brows. He imagined a girl with a cleft palate, narrow eyes, and a slack mouth—but with Suzanne's straight dark hair, Suzanne's grumpy, thoughtful, and amused expressions. If the baby were a girl, they'd name her Hope Louise Casterlin, for Adam's late mother, Louise. "It'll be great to worry about our child's sex life someday," he said.

When Suzanne smiled, he imagined that smile on their child's face.

Whatever their baby's future might be, they could accept it, but who would the baby take after? Could any child of hers also resemble him? She was the director of finance at a publishing house. She'd supported him through grad school. Her corrections of his dissertation—he'd misspelled a word in the title—won him a tenure-track job. She'd prompted him, line by line, through the personal vows he'd dreamed up but bungled for their wedding. "Marriage is your last, best chance to grow up," the minister had said, and all of Adam's friends had laughed. Nobody was surprised that he was the one crying at the altar, with the maid of honor passing him tissues.

When she said they should wait until they were thirty to have kids, he had suppressed his eagerness for a family, as well as his suspicion that, relying so much on her, he hadn't grown up at all. For all his success, he felt more like a child than ever. Didn't people remain children until they had children of their own?

On his thirtieth birthday, she'd rewarded his patience. "Let's have a baby," she'd finally said. They were eating dessert at his favorite restaurant. He had swallowed his mouthful of cake, felt solemn and confused, and touched her hand. It was only late that night, after they'd gone to bed, after an episode of shy, stately formality, then hysterical laughter, that he realized she had given him something else, too. She'd been right to delay until she wanted the baby as much as he did. She had restored his faith in her decisions and shown him that his faith in her was the greatest of his own assets.

Then they turned thirty-one, and thirty-two, and forty. It was only after they'd bought a white carpet and resigned themselves to the quiescence of middle age that she missed a period. "It's probably a hormonal surge," she said. Neither of them could say the words "early menopause." And so when she burst into the doctor's reception room after her exam, crying out the news, he'd cried too, and trembled, holding her gingerly as though she might break. She had had to drive them home, though he kept insisting, "Slow down! Be careful!"

He bought a handmade paper album with gilt-edged pages.

In gold ink he headed the first page, "Week One, Day One: Fertilization," and charted out the baby's history. Previously he had recorded Suzanne's ovulation calendar; now he downloaded photos and diagrams of zygotes and fetuses to accompany each entry. Today, heartbeats. Today, arm budding. Today, tooth formation in the jawbones. Today—identifiable fingerprints! For the first time he understood why pro-lifers reckoned life from conception: the actual birth, so far in the future, could hardly rival the thrill of seeing a ball of cells curl into baby shape.

He also recorded the changes in Suzanne. He had never before been so aware of her body, not when he'd fallen in love, not when they'd married. At forty-one, she was radiant and unfamiliar. Her skin flushed with capillary growth to conduct more oxygen to the placenta; her hair grew oily and glossy; even her chewing was turning food into *baby*. Sometimes she resembled a stick insect bulging with eggs. She'd started to stomp when she walked, and she smelled a little different.

He had feared that his desire would fail, that he'd find her pregnancy foreign and repulsive, though he professionally questioned the constructs of foreignness and repulsion. But sex was now truly sensuous and abandoned: no more thermometers or jerking off into specimen jars. No more guilt about missing a scheduled sex act, because their fertility treatments cost so much. Even her embarrassment about her morning sickness seemed intimate, after the years without any privacy.

Her pregnancy stimulated his admiration as well as his protective urge. Such fortitude, such tenacity, vomiting every morning and relocating her bones to increase pelvic capacity! Although he had associated pregnancy with beatific placidity, like Renoir's women, she dreaded the nausea and raged against her chronic lassitude. She struggled to keep up her routines of yoga and overtime at work, but her body's new demands prevailed.

He learned to make small mistakes around the house, in the checkbook, just so she could correct him. When she cried fretfully about her vulnerability, he held her and soothed her. He told her that she was strong, she had always been the strong one, and everything would soon return to normal.

She sighed, "You're going to be such a good father." They had waited over a decade for this pregnancy, and if he couldn't carry the baby, he could help carry Suzanne.

Week 17, Day 117. They'd grown accustomed to doctors younger than they were, and Dr. Collier with her pageboy and soft handshake might be a little girl playing dress-up. The ultrasound technician, Heather, had braces, and was surely too young to be twiddling the monitor and gliding the transducer over Suzanne's abdomen.

Mission Control, do you read me, Houston? Adam thought. And there it was, pinpointed on the screen, crackling like a radio message from space: translucent whites and grays blurred on black, like the moon. The dark craters of eyes, a ghostly face just beneath Suzanne's navel, beneath Adam's fingers, yet so far away: a little man—or woman—in the moon, gazing back at them.

Like the first lunar landing. He had been five, riveted at first by the TV images, then disappointed by the lack of rocket battles and green oozing things. Now he remembered the excitement building up to the lunar broadcast, the thrill of incredible distances brought into his parents' living room.

She squeezed his hand. The screen image jumped. "The baby... it felt...!" he stuttered.

She cried, "It felt us! It knew we were touching."

"Week 17, Day 117: Umbilical cord," he'd write. That was the name of the astronauts' air and communications cable during moonwalk. He would decorate the album pages with photos of the landing and their ultrasound prints. He would paint the nursery midnight blue with shooting stars and planets. Spinning giddily inside, tethered only by Suzanne's grip on his hand, and, through her, to the baby floating in the dark, he heard her ask, "Is it a boy or girl?"

Dr. Collier was smiling too. "I don't have a good view of a penis, so it might be a girl, but the amnio will tell us for sure."

If it's a girl, we'll name her Hope Louise Sally Ride Casterlin, Adam thought.

Heather the technician said, "Okay, let's get a better image here. Okay. O-kay. All right...." Her voice trailed off as she squinted into the screen.

"What's going on?" Suzanne said.

"Nothing," the doctor said, shooting a warning glance at Heather. That look was the first bad moment.

Suzanne said, "Am I blocking it somehow? Should I move?"

Heather maneuvered the transducer, while Suzanne lay holding her breath. Adam stared at the screen. He saw the baby's glimmering face. But where there should have been an expanse of forehead, there was only blackness. Dr. Collier offered them a drink of water and asked permission for her and Heather to step outside for a moment.

When they'd closed the door, Suzanne asked him, "What is it?"

"I don't know. It looks like, like..." It looked like nothing. "Is it a—" he groped for words, rejected *tumor*, "a growth of some kind?"

"It can't be," she said decisively. "Growths are just more tissue. A growth would look white, not dark. It must be some kind of technical problem. I knew we shouldn't have come."

Dr. Collier returned alone and said in a bedside tone, "Suzanne, I'd like to take a blood sample to clarify the reading, while

Heather's doing the prints."

Adam's stomach plummeted. He said, "What about the amnio? Don't we need the amnio?" It was important to reestablish the simple reason they'd come here.

Dr. Collier said, "The alpha-betoprotein screening is the only test we need right now."

"Is there some kind of technical problem?" Suzanne asked.

"I don't think—"

"I know it's not a *growth*."

Dr. Collier said gently, "We just need to rule out all the possibilities."

Suzanne didn't wince at the needle; she'd endured so many. After they'd cleaned up, she dressed, climbed off the examination couch, and was seated in a chair in the private waiting room. Wanting to hold her hand, but feeling that the gesture would bespeak an unnecessary anxiety, he sat, cracking his knuckles, until finally she enfolded his hands in hers.

When Dr. Collier had returned and laid the prints on the table before them, she talked for a long time. Adam heard and didn't hear her words: *neural tube disorder, tissue erosion, sympathy, hemorrhage, folic acid, counselor, spina bifida, stillbirth, mortality, anencephaly.* They made no sense. He said, "Are you saying our baby has spina bifida?" He willed Suzanne to look at him, thinking, *we can deal with this, we only need to prepare,* but she was staring at the prints.

Dr. Collier said, "The fetus has no brain. I am so sorry to have to tell you this."

Adam said, "But we saw her—its—the baby's face. It was perfectly normal." His words were coming out wrong. Couldn't Dr. Collier at least tell them if the baby were a boy or girl?

Dr. Collier was saying that they should schedule an induction immediately. Suzanne looked up for the first time. She said,

"You mean an abortion?"

While the doctor explained the possible complications and the staffing of the procedure, everything became stupidly clear to Adam. He knew it; he'd taught it in his Intro to Social Change class: there was no such thing as a potential human being. There were fetuses, and only after birth were there babies. It was fetuses, not babies, which were aborted.

Suzanne said, "I would have to deliver the baby? In labor?"

Dr. Collier said, "D and E—that's dilation and evacuation—is physically less traumatic, but we don't perform second-trimester D and E here. With induction, the fetus is expelled by uterine contractions induced by a solution of saline and prostaglandin."

Suzanne said, "But, but couldn't the baby be born? Alive?"

Dr. Collier said, "Signs of life are extremely rare after an induction."

"I mean, what if we don't have an induction? If we just go on?"

Dr. Collier said softly, "There is no real viability outside the womb. The fetus might die even before coming to term, or be delivered in stillbirth. Even if it survived labor, it could live only a few minutes, maybe up to an hour." She gave them a folder full of documents and pamphlets. "But there is no hope. This isn't just a birth defect. The condition is absolutely incompatible with life."

Suzanne said, "Adam?"

He knew something was required of him, but he couldn't respond.

Dr. Collier said, "I want to schedule an appointment for you to come back tomorrow to talk more about the procedure and speak with our counselor. But for now, go home and get some rest, if you can. Please call me with any questions. I am so very sorry."

Suzanne said, "Where is our video?" Dr. Collier hesitated. "We want it now."

"All right." The doctor pulled the door close, but they could hear her, in the hallway, asking for the video. Somebody said, "The residents are watching it." Dr. Collier said, "We need to give it back, immediately."

Suzanne said, "What are we going to do? Adam?"

Adam stood and clasped Suzanne's hands in his, to raise her from the couch. But then her head and arms sagged, like pricked balloons, and he couldn't pull without hurting her. He bent over her, feeling that any moment his own strength would fail and they'd have to stay slumped in this waiting room forever.

She called out sick from work. He spoke to his department head and cancelled his classes. His calls went straight to voicemail, and he relied on his T.A. to respond to his students. His friends left cheerful e-mails, then, as his silence lengthened, increasingly nervous ones. "Hey Adam, haven't heard from you for a while. Has your server gone down?"

He had kept the pregnancy a secret from everybody, exulting privately with Suzanne. After all the strain, the silence, and sometimes the crude, awkward jokes—*Are you shooting blanks? Hey, relax, you two are trying too hard*; unbelievable things that the kindest, best-intentioned people couldn't help saying to them, trying to lighten the grief—he couldn't have borne the ecstatic congratulations, the uproar, and, most of all, his friends' and family's relief. Nobody had truly shared their burden; nobody could understand their success. But if he'd thought before that his tongue was tied... Even his father called. "Your sisters say they haven't heard from you in a while. How's Suzy-Q?"

"Suzy-Q" was a recent development. When he and Suzanne had first married, his mother had said, "A lot of young women seem to support their families nowadays, but you have a good job now. Suzanne doesn't have to work anymore." They were setting the table for Easter brunch; Suzanne was hiding eggs outside for Adam's nieces and nephews.

"Mom, if one of us stayed home, it'd be me."

"Doesn't she want to raise her own kids?" Louise had said.

"We're not sure we want kids."

His mother had prodded, "*We?* Don't you mean Suzanne's not sure?"

"I don't think that I'm ready to be a father."

Louise had said, "You mean Suzanne doesn't think you're ready."

It was true that he'd felt, sometimes, that Suzanne was waiting for him to pass some maturity test before she'd entrust him with fatherhood. That stung a little. But he'd loyally told his mother, "Suzy isn't ready, either. She knows what it's like when people have children they're not ready to raise. She doesn't want to treat her kids the way she was treated."

"Adam, a parent is never, ever ready to have kids. You can't prepare for everything that can go wrong. You can only hope for the best. So don't wait until it's too late."

Adam had felt more irritated with his mother than he had since he was a teenager grounded for sneaking out at night. "Like I said, we'll do it when we're ready, Mom."

She had rubbed his back. "I know, honey. I don't mean to nag. It's just that I love you and your sisters more than anything, and I want you to experience that feeling for yourselves someday. It's like no other love you'll ever have. It'll change your world. You and Suzanne shouldn't miss out on it."

One time, after they'd started their fertility treatments, Adam and Suzanne took his parents out for Mother's Day. The waiter had passed around their menus, and then to Louise, "For you, Madame," a white rose in a vase. "And for you," another for Suzanne. They all had looked around the room to see families at other tables. Each mother had been given a white rose. With a stricken expression, Suzanne had laid down her menu and excused herself to the restroom. Louise had looked hard after her, then at Adam, who met her glance, then looked away. He felt that he should have shared his hopes with her—but he hadn't had the words at his disposal. Then, when their plans began to go awry, he had been too embarrassed, too upset. Louise called the waiter to have both vases removed. When Suzanne returned to the table, outwardly unruffled, but too quiet, Louise touched her hand, one quick hard squeeze, then busily passed around the bread.

After that day, his family had tried to avoid the subject at holiday gatherings, but what was there to chat about except his nieces' and nephews' nursery schools, allergies, and discipline problems? Louise had learned to inquire about Suzanne's work with the specificity and enthusiasm she usually reserved for her grandchildren. During those conversations, Adam had wanted to scream. *You accept her only now that we've tried and failed. Our personal best is only second-rate. We don't need your pity or your acceptance.*

But when Suzanne finally got pregnant, there was only one person he had wanted to tell: his mother, then dead for two years. He had wanted to show her a different, maternal Suzanne, who was knitting a layette and drinking gallons of milk. He had wanted the two of them to confer over baby clothes; argue about Lamaze, multivitamins, and breastfeeding; side against him on the midwifery issue. He had wanted to tell Louise, *I know now what you were saying. We have the love you wanted us to have. No matter what my child chooses to do with its life, no matter what its personal best is, I will accept it for who it is.*

They returned to the hospital to talk with the counselor. He asked about their religious beliefs. Suzanne shook her head. "We're not religious," Adam said.

The counselor said, "You must understand that any expectation you have of bonding with a living baby will be impossible."

Dr. Collier said, "You have to do this as soon as possible. Your risk grows every day."

They learned that the fetus was female.

Suzanne said, "I need to talk it over with Adam."

They didn't talk at all. At night she stared at the TV, oblivious to commercials and his channel flipping. In the mornings she slept through the alarm. He knew that whatever exhaustion, anger, and grief he felt, her feelings were even more terrible; that he could offer no support or comfort she could find acceptable; that she would think, and grieve, alone, and emerge from her solitude only when she was ready to act. That was how she was. But he wanted to be together. Their doctors had always warned them not to let infertility destroy their marriage. He wouldn't let them be destroyed now.

One night he watched Suzanne forcing down some rice and beans that had grown cold on her plate. He grabbed the keys and drove to the supermarket to buy a boxed brownie mix, her favorite. By the time he'd returned, she'd eaten only a few more bites. "I'm making you brownies," he said. Still wearing his coat, he got out the oil and eggs and preheated the oven.

She looked bewildered. "What are you doing?"

"I'm making you some brownies," he repeated, ripping the top off the box.

She said, "We're not supposed to eat sugar or chocolate."

"You've lost your appetite. You love brownies more than anything else in the world, so I'm making you some. Just one, it won't hurt you." This taste of sweetness was his gift to her, just the smallest stupid gesture to show her that he loved her and was helpless before her pain.

She said slowly, "They're not healthy for the baby."

He stood staring at her, a cracked egg in his hand. The white slipped through his fingers into a pool atop the brownie mix.

She said, "I can't have the induction. I'm carrying the baby to term."

"But it's not a baby, it's a fetus," he said numbly.

"Why does everybody keep *saying* that?"

"I'm sorry!" They'd just been talking about brownies, when she'd gone and said *baby*. Now he had hurt her. He regretted it, but it was the truth, wasn't it? "Dr. Collier made it very clear that the baby won't make it. It might not even make it so far as the ninth month. I can't believe that she'll let you go through with this."

"She won't. It's not 'procedure,' she says."

"You...you called her? You talked it over with her already?"

She hesitated. "Yes. I have to use another hospital," she said.

He struggled to make sense of it all. "Suzy. I want a baby just as much as you do. But we have to think about it in terms of the next one. We'll be forty-two; we can't afford to wait. Every day we wait, we're making that healthy baby wait, too."

She said, "Have you forgotten what it was like? The mucus swabs and thermometers, and all those doctors saying, 'Oops, better luck on the next go-round'?"

"I haven't forgotten! That's why we have to start now! We have another chance for another baby."

She said, "What if this is the only baby we have? How can you give up the chance to hold your own baby in your arms, even if you only get five minutes? Can you promise me that it'll work next time? Can you promise me that we'll even get another chance?"

There was nothing he could say. He busied himself with dropping in the yolk and mixing. The whisk clattered in the silence of their kitchen.

"I thought so. You're hopeless," she said, and left.

He waited until he heard her running a bath. Then he tipped the batter into the sink and rinsed it down the drain.

He entered his study for the first time since the ultrasound, and saw the album and his computer print-outs. Photos he'd meant to paste in: Suzanne teaching herself to knit; Suzanne taking notes as Carmen explained something; Suzanne in the bath; Suzanne queasily eating applesauce for breakfast, and the caption, "Week 11, Day 73—*Put down the goddamn camera!*" A photo of Adam himself, gaping at the flash when Suzanne had sneaked up on him. He was surrounded by ribbons, calligraphy pens, and pastel stickers, making the album for their child to bring to Show and Tell.

He saw the detritus of his expectations, dust, ungraded midterms, and unpaid bills. Meanwhile, she had been busy.

He turned on his computer and went online, as he had done before, to find articles and pictures. Only this time, he found photos of babies born bruised and battered, bleeding from their open skulls. Exposed spinal nubs and abscesses. Because their poor heads were too soft to push through the birth canal, they had to be delivered by cesarean. Did Suzanne know this? Did she know what birth would do to her, as well as to the baby? Pity, for himself, for Suzanne, for all the babies, overwhelmed him.

Of course she doesn't know; that's why you have to tell her. He felt like a pro-lifer with one of those gruesome, manipulative placards. It was cruel, using intimidation and disgust to overcome her reason and limit her choices. His own participation in the pregnancy had been an illusion. The fetus did not share his breath, his eating or drinking, his anxiety, his health. Fatherhood was an imaginative act—Athena springing from Zeus's head—but it was a void, and imagination an empty thing. Fatherhood had meant repletion, happiness expanding inside him until he thought he would burst, and work, too: hours of reading, planning, and caring for Suzanne. But as the joy had been a trick of the brain, so must be its loss. He wouldn't bear any stretch marks.

As for the album, he couldn't keep it, not even as a memento, because it lied. Their tiny embryo had nearly resembled the ones in the photos, with its coral-like branching of blood vessels and unraveling shrimp shape. But there was nothing in the album to explain why on Day 28 its neural tube had failed to close, its skull laid open, and the brain bud, if it had had any, eroded. He would destroy the album on the day of the induction. In the meantime, he hid it away in a file cabinet.

He had read about a man who killed his girlfriend's child and hid it in the dumpster behind their apartment. When the police questioned him, he said, "Baby? What baby?"

What baby?

Morning. Seated on the couch, staring at his socked feet, he heard her run for the bathroom. A choke. A light spatter. Nothing much ever came up; she'd said once that it would be a relief to bring up more, to produce something from all that wracked tension. Carmen had said that morning sickness was correlated to fetal health: nausea prevented overexertion and limited expectant mothers' diets to only the blandest, safest foods.

He swallowed, and slid his right foot into the shoe. *She's sick because it's pushing her stomach aside to make more room for itself. Its bloodstream is crawling with hormones that screw with her metabolism. It's like a parasite.* He felt ill too. He thought, *Freak.* He hung his head between his knees. It wasn't just a nightmare. It was happening in his house, in his bed: a fetus fattening, its limbs spreading, its thumb stuck instinctively, unknowingly, into its mouth. Its cells were multiplying, but to what end?

He heard her washing up, then her pacing around the house until she found him. She wore a beautifully tailored tweed maternity suit. "What are you doing?" she asked.

He sat up. "Putting on my shoes." Silence. He looked up; her belly was at his eye level. "I'd better get going."

She folded her arms. "What's wrong?"

"Nothing. I've got early office hours today."

A patient, wifely, inexorable smile. "Adam."

He said, "You throw up all the time. Don't you want to feel better? Don't you want to stop suffering like this?"

She shrugged. "It's not that bad. It's natural."

He said, "It is not natural, Suzanne." He stared at the knots in his shoelaces. "You marched with NARAL in Washington. You were uncomfortable about having a Down Syndrome baby. Yet you're willing to carry this one for four more months, only for it to be a terrible experience, no dignity at all, just pain and machines and doctors and—all for it to die in the end."

She said, "That's an obnoxious way to put it."

Hopeless, she had called him. But hope was stupid and dangerous. Hope was about putting your fantasies above common sense, above everybody else's needs. He said, "It's the realistic, fair way to put it. You aren't thinking. You're supposed to be so smart, so capable, but you're acting like, like...." Now that he'd come to it, he couldn't say what he needed to say.

"I know what I want to do."

"But I don't want to do it!" he said.

She said, "You don't have to do anything! It's not your decision."

He remembered wanting to shield her from the truth. He remembered his attempts to subordinate his feelings to hers. She had thrown it all back in his face. "Are you really saying that to me, after all we went through?" She was silent. He said, "I've seen photos of these babies when people actually give birth to them, Suzanne. They're terrible. I didn't want to show them to you, but I will, just to make you see how horrible and misguided your ideas are."

"I've seen the pictures. Do you think you're the only one capable of doing Internet research?" she said. "You sit there, with your rubber cement and scissors, going on Google, and this puts you in the know? When have you ever made a decision on your own or taken up your share of the responsibilities in this marriage? And now you think you've figured out what's best for me and the baby? You think you've solved our problems? It's a little late for you to start *thinking*, Adam!"

Everything she'd said was true, and no worse than the insults he'd imagined for himself in the past. But he held the trump card. "I may not be the smart one in this marriage, but at least I wouldn't put a baby through so much pain just so I could hold it for five minutes!"

She said, "What pain? Have you forgotten that it doesn't have a brain?"

Their marriage seemed no more than the frame that contained their mutual loathing. It was all that would be left, tattered and diminished, after the birth. He no longer believed in her. Dully, he wondered how she had managed to believe in him, all these years. He said, "I can't explain it to you, but what you're doing is so wrong it's unforgivable. If our marriage depends on your reasoning, then we've reached the place where I can't go along with it anymore."

"I didn't ask you to go along with my decision," she said. "And I'll drive myself to work." That was that.

A few evenings later, he came home from work to find her waiting in the living room. She'd been crying. Around her were stacks of gift boxes straggling bright ribbons. A wooden rocking horse stood beside a stroller and a car seat. She said, "Adam, please don't say anything until I can explain. I had no idea this was going to happen. They took me into the conference room. They'd bought balloons and streamers." She picked up a box and set it down again. "And a cake shaped like a teddy bear. I started to cry. I said it was tears of joy."

He opened the nearest box: Winnie the Pooh dishes. Another box: a miniature yellow slicker, with reflective trim, and tiny Wellington boots. A Gund panda named Bei Bei. Who would give an animal that refused to breed to a baby who'd been eleven years in the making?

She said, "Carolyn and Jerry came home with me to get the heavy things inside. She asked to see the nursery. I said it had just been painted and the fumes were too bad. They said that they were all so happy for us that they couldn't resist throwing a shower, even though it was so early. They know how hard it's been, waiting. I couldn't tell them what was happening, not then. Adam, I couldn't tell them to return their presents. I don't even know if they kept receipts. I don't know what to do."

There were heavy silver items, a cup, rattle, and picture frames. He imagined Suzanne in a beribboned desk chair, opening packages, exclaiming over the delicate shoes, basking in the attention. Being a mother. He strove to sound calm. "Well, you'll figure something out."

"Can't you.... Is that all you have to say?"

"What do you want me to say? I thought this was the Immaculate Conception! It's not like I have any say in the matter, is it?"

"I knew you'd be upset, but what could I do?"

He said, "You know exactly what you could do about it!" He looked at the furniture, the children's books, and the clothes in genderless primary colors. The collection of silver. He said, "It's a thing with things now."

Just when he'd thought that she had done the most awful

thing she could, she hissed, "She is not a thing, her name is Hope Louise."

Hope Louise. He shouted, "You are not naming it after my mother!"

"Your mother hated me! You're the one who wanted to name it after her!" She clutched her belly with one hand, and he felt, simply, hatred. Hatred for the layette, for her maternal gestures, for the thing inside her, everything.

"You only give names to babies! This isn't a baby, it's a deformity! How can you stand to give *birth* to it? Anyone decent would put it out of its misery!"

Her face contorted in rage. Then she gasped, and wrapped her arms around her body, hands pressed to her sides. She bent over, her face drawn, unseeing, concentrating on the thing.

Against his will, he felt his old love and his endless preoccupation with Suzanne entwine with his anger. He said, "What is it? Are you all right?"

"Leave me alone!" She shut herself in the bathroom.

It was he who had insisted on a big white church wedding. Suzanne had wanted only a civil service and a return to their normal lives. Their wedding was more than ritual display to him; it had been something real for him to look forward to and realize. So he had learned how to keep house, hold down a job, be a husband. So he had charted her calendar. So he had created the baby's album. So, on their anniversary this year, when Suzanne was two months pregnant, he had bought her three dozen pink roses and toasted her with sparkling grape juice. Their home was suffused with the scent of roses. The next morning the smell had made her sick, so he'd had to put the roses out on the porch.

He'd thrown himself onto the bed without bothering to turn out any lights. Around ten, she joined him. He pretended to be asleep. There was a soft clicking noise. He peeked at her: she sat propped against the pillows, knitting fine yellow lambswool.

The clicking stopped. "Adam," she said, "give me your hand." She had known he was awake. She bundled up her t-shirt and laid his hand flat against her abdomen. She said, "Wait."

He waited, feeling nothing but the rise and fall of her breathing.

Then something poked him. He recoiled. He stared at the smooth, round mound and tentatively replaced his hand. Poke.

Suzanne said, "She's kicking. Or elbowing me." Smoothness again, then the faintest ripple under the skin. "And turning over, I think."

"What does it feel like?"

"It's like a finger snapped on your skin. Or, when it gets up under my ribs, it's like a noogie."

He said, "When did it start?"

"When we were fighting. She kicked once, then twice. I couldn't believe it." Her gaze was steady. "But she's *kicking*."

He thought of the rice, beans, applesauce, and milk; the blood, water, and oxygen; the flesh, the genes, the tests charts thermometers tubes clocks swabs frustration fear fucking love—everything that had gone into the making of these vibrations under his hand. He felt the kicking and knew it was only a reflex, a neural glitch produced by the spinal cord, like suckling, like blinking, like everything else that babies were supposed to do. All these things—the growth, the anticipation, the kicking, the rooting in deeper—were their child's portion in life, its personal best.

And his portion was to tell it, *Thank you so much for doing this for us. You don't have to prove yourself any longer. You were ours for a little while—but now you can stop. You don't need to be born, blind and deaf and still, only to die for us.* He had to resist his own incompetence and cowardice, holding to the fact that for once in his life, he was right. Even if it drove her away from him, he could never accept her decision. If he failed in his love, he would have to learn to live without it.

She had picked up her knitting again. He said, "What are you making?"

"A hat." A cap the size of a peach. "I've got eight rows left."

He remembered the ultrasound. He remembered the black eyes, large and watchful. He remembered the astronaut's umbilical. Once the baby was born and the cord delivered with the placenta, its oxygen would be cut off. Its lungs would never fill with air. *Mayday, Mission Control.*

He remembered the darkness above its half-skull. "Finish off that row."

"But it's not the right size yet," she said, glancing at the instructions.

He said, "Suzanne. It's just the right size."

She frowned. Then the needles fell from her hands. And when her head pressed against his chest, hard and heavy, he wondered if that was what it felt like, the dead weight she carried.

⚐ *In the Tradition of My Family* ⚐
PHIL LAMARCHE

In the tradition of my family I was shot at the age of thirteen. My father, lacking a zeal for familial custom, chose to send a small caliber round through the flesh connecting two of my toes. While this placement saved me from some immediate discomfort, it was a terrible burden for the rest of my teenage years. At family events, when the men met and disrobed, amidst the leering of uncles and cousins, I worked my toes apart for the scar to be seen.

⚐

Cousin Eldridge was shot with a thirty-thirty at close range. The large, fleshy deposit of scar tissue on the underside of his shoulder bears the satellite pocks of powder burn. His father, Uncle Jess, has a similar scar between his shoulder and neck. It was the son, and not the father, who requested the same firearm at a similar distance. At family events the two sit shirtless, side by side. I was envious of Eldridge, as my father rarely attended such occasions, and I sat alone—a shoe and sock the only articles of clothing I was required to remove.

I did not make any requests of my father prior to the day of my shooting, so perhaps I am as much to blame. That day, I woke, and went to the shed to wait. It was several hours before he arrived and I must admit my disappointment at seeing the small carbine he sometimes used to extinguish the bothersome floodlights of neighboring homes. He was known for his marksmanship and for a moment I hoped for some surgical placement that narrowly avoided my heart and lungs. A scar, no matter how small, can be dignified if prominently displayed. My great-grandfather, only having access to a short-barreled gambler's pistol during the years of the Depression, put the firearm to the side of his boy's face, instructed him to open his mouth, and shot him through both cheeks. The resulting scars are some of the most distinguished in the family.

When I neared thirteen I woke each morning hoping to hear my grandfather had died. I wanted the odd, misplaced dimples for myself. No one would dare replicate them unless it was in memory, and the ailing old man kept breathing. Instead, in the shed, my father told me to remove my shoe. Sock as well, he said. He had me place my foot on a large bag of potting soil. He told me to cover my ears. It was as quick as I had been promised.

He hoisted me back to my feet, slung me over his shoulder, and carried me inside to the couch. My mother was furious. Not so furious that she didn't pack my foot in ice, but I could hear her berating my father through the closed doors of our house. A door opened and my father came into the room. She continued yelling from the kitchen.

"In the shoulder," she said. "Your own brother, never to use so much as a shovel again." He stopped but he would not look at me. "Benjamin," she said. "He won't even have a limp to show for it." My father left the room.

She wanted him to take me out to the shed and shoot again. She said we could hide the first one, we could tell the rest of the family I had stubbed my toe.

"Besides," she said from the kitchen. "With all their attention on a proper wound they'll never notice the foot." When my father failed to reply she entered the room and scanned for his presence. Not finding him, she shook her head in disgust, returning to ready the kitchen for the oncoming crowd.

The family arrived shortly. My uncles bore large bowls of assorted salads and crocks of casserole. My aunts carried fresh dressings for my wound and bags of ice to stem any swelling. My cousins toted small wrapped gifts. Their excitement waned when my mother refused to show them. She told them the wound was still fresh and needed to clot. But when she was in the kitchen, getting utensils to serve the food, several of my aunts and female cousins, giddy with anticipation, set to undressing my foot. They had rags torn from old t-shirts, ointment in tin tubes, fresh gauze and rolls of white medical tape.

At the sight of my foot, Aunt Elize began to cry. This made me cry. My uncles and cousins congregated. They could not hide their disappointment. Uncle Aldous turned and walked away. Uncle Henry followed him. They went to a corner to whisper a conversation. About the time my cousin Charles was pointing and laughing, my mother came out of the kitchen and did her best to disperse the crowd. She threw a dish towel over my bare foot and ushered people into the dining room. I continued to cry and no one tried to stop me.

My mother took my uncle Jess by the elbow before he had a chance to leave the room.

"Can you do something?" she asked him. He looked at me and I could tell he wanted to do something. I grew warm with the thought of the two of us alone in the shed. I stopped crying.

"Suppose he expects the right to one of my sons," Uncle Jess said. "Suppose he then does this to one of mine. No," he said.

"Please," said my mother.

"I can do nothing," he told her. "I'm sorry."

My mother insisted the events of the day go accordingly—the

men disrobed, the women cleaned and dressed my wound, the children filed passed, leaving their gifts before me—but it lacked any air of celebration. I was disgracefully conscious for the duration. The day is usually spent with the new-man drifting in and out, sweating, deliriously repeating statements of gratitude. I sat upright and alert. Instead of the traditional fare of the severely wounded—the sweet breads, wine and white-bean porridge—I ate cheese-balls and drank grape soda.

We did skip the custom of the partially dressed men reciting the stories of their own shootings. The women assisted in these tales, telling of how difficult it had been to curtail the fevers, how persistent the blood loss had been, what nonsense the new-men had spoken in their deliriums. Aunt Elize cackles away every time she tells of how her son Elderidge, bedridden for days, had begged her, *Please can I lie down? I'm so tired of standing.*

Instead of the stories, they spoke of a television show it seemed they all had seen the night before. By then, I was trying to fake my own unconsciousness, my own deliriums, but they seemed not to notice. While the adults spoke, the children made their way around the circle of men, running their fingers over the knots of hardened flesh that had been revealed. The men occasionally twitched and shivered. They say you can see the finger touching the scar, can even feel the pressure of it there, but only rarely does the tickle of flesh against flesh seep through. After my own wound had healed I would pull my toes apart and attempt to experience this for myself.

Before the visit ended, Uncle Aldous crouched beside me. He surveyed the room and waited a moment more before whispering in my ear.

"I suppose that you, more than any of us, wonder why your father would choose to disgrace you."

I nodded, comforted by the alliance his position and tone created between us.

"I must remind you it would be inappropriate for you to question him."

I nodded again.

"But we are your family, boy. Your uncles and I will look into this." Aldous scanned the room again. "For the life of me I cannot understand him."

"He feels above us," Elize squawked.

Aldous held a finger to his lips, but Elize did not heed.

"His whole life," she said. "Not having to disrobe. It might've done the same to you."

"And father?" said Aldous in a raised whisper. "Never disrobed a day in his life."

"A man of greater character," Elize said.

"If you care to insult my husband I'd appreciate you not doing it here."

Elize did not turn to face my mother. She lowered her head and nodded. The room was silent except for several children tumbling about in a corner.

There is no need for my father to disrobe. When it was his time, he was told to hold his hands together, palm to palm. My grandfather did his best to shoot between the bones of the first hand, but when it came to the second, the bullet had strayed. To make a fist he must use his good hand to fold the other fingers in.

His hands out flat, the scars on the backsides are in opposition. One being the entry, the other an exit. On the back of the right there is an indentation, much smaller than the dome of flesh that rises from the left. It looks as though someone took their time, carefully pouring the drippings of a candle, letting each layer cool before adding another and another. When he lays his hands on the dinner table, everyone knows he is his father's oldest and most favored son.

Shortly after the family departed, my father returned. He sat in the chair next to me, the two of us silent in front of the television.

"It is they who suffer," said my father. "Swollen in such a way with themselves."

I strained my eyes sideways to see him. I would not turn my head for fear that he would as well—I could not bear to look him in the eye. I was his only son. I cannot say that I even knew the man but I had thought certain things compulsory between us. I had been dutiful.

There was the sound of the television and the noise of my mother cleaning up in the kitchen—the clanks of bowls and dishes mitigated by the wall and door between us.

"It has always been intended to instill virtue." He was looking at me. I could just make out the whites of his eyes.

I began crying again.

"I'm sorry you don't understand," he said.

He stood and left the room. I heard the front door open and close. When my mother entered and inquired, I told her that my foot throbbed. The truth was that my foot had been on ice for so long that I could feel nothing of it. There were moments when I could pretend it was gone, the shooting having taken it entirely.

᭡

I cannot say that I yet understand him. It could be said he wished to avoid the pain, the jeopardy to my life—we have lost several to the shootings in my lifetime alone—but he had, and has not since expressed a concern for my physical well being. I was given sharp cutlery as a youth, never required to wear a helmet on a bicycle, and never encouraged to wear a seatbelt. Early in my teens

I was introduced to cigarettes and alcohol without my father's objection.

Having grown and learned little more of my father I assume it was his attempt at teaching me something grand. He pulled the trigger on the flesh between my toes to say: *See, it all means nothing. They are fools.* But it is treacherous for a man with the most dignified scars of his generation to point to their superficiality, as it is for a rich man to advocate the virtue of the poor.

*

At fifteen I arrived at a family gathering stoned and reeking of alcohol. When it was time for us to disrobe, I clumsily kicked off my shoe and then with a mocking air of gusto, I threw my sock over my shoulder. My father was not present to witness this. Uncle Aldous took a seat at my side and leaned in to me.

"I will not have this," he said. "I would rather your blood upon my hands than have you continue in this manner."

I knew he meant it. Unlike my father, Aldous would not insult me with a flesh wound. His threat filled me with warmth. I began to cry and Aldous slapped me. I kept sobbing and he continued hitting me—hard, opened handed, high on my cheek. He relented only when my body had ceased convulsing. I accepted the last several blows with my jaw set, my eyes locked with his. I so wished to call him father. Together we turned back to the circle of men. It was then that I realized the love that surrounded me.

*

I visit my mother on Tuesday afternoons. As my father stares blankly at the television, my mother and I drink coffee at the kitchen table. She is happy that I have not moved away. She is happy that I have not married any of the women I have been involved with thus far.

She is not right for us, my mother has said with each of them. *She will never understand.*

"Was it difficult for you?" I ask her.

"Nothing is so hard when you are dutiful," she tells me. "You are a responsible man. You must find a responsible woman."

"They're different now," I say.

"They were different then," she says. "But there will always be women of virtue."

"Did it scare you?" I ask her.

"How could it?" she says. "His hands were what I first fell in love with."

❧

One of my father's few paternal gestures in my childhood was to buy me a dog. It was a mongrel of no particular value but as children do, I grew very attached to it. I believe I cared for it adequately, but several years later it was struck by a car in the street before our home. Of course the car did not stop, such is the sense of duty in our world. I found the dog on the back porch, where it had dragged itself, licking its useless hind legs. I ran and brought my father. Seeing its state he went back in the house and returned with a blanket. He wrapped the dog and carried it out behind the shed where he gently set it down.

"Stay," he told me. "Make sure to tell him what you think of him."

He returned with the small carbine that he would join me in the shed with several years later. He handed me the rifle and two bullets.

"You shouldn't need both," he said.

I stared at him. I didn't say anything.

"You owe him this," he told me.

I looked to the dog. He looked bored. He was panting on the blanket and I doubted the necessity of my father's proposition. He must have seen my indecision.

"Do you want me to do it?" said my father, hastily grabbing at the barrel of the carbine. I held the rifle firm and shook my head. "Good," he said. "I'll be inside."

I positioned myself in a way that I wouldn't have to see his eyes.

"This doesn't mean you did anything wrong," I whispered. "They say it gets better."

I took aim on the back of his head and fired. He nuzzled his face into the blanket as if trying to rub an itch on his muzzle, but shortly quit. His skin twitched slightly but even that soon ceased. I ejected the spent shell and then the unfired bullet, placing both in my pocket.

Together, my father and I burned a fire through the afternoon, into night. We tossed the carcass onto the coal-bed and retreated to the house. I slept little and in the morning I rushed to find that my father had already turned the remains into the soil. I wanted to see the skull, the teeth, the burned-black portions of body that resisted fire. Instead I found a rustled section of dirt—something that could have been the beginnings of a garden. I kicked through it, but found nothing of the dog.

❧

After we finish our coffee, I leave my mother in the kitchen. In the next room I look at the silhouette of my father's head, hung in sleep—a small, black half-circle rising above the back of his recliner. The glow of the television fluctuates from around his darkness. The light flashes in the glass of the gun cabinet across the room. The carbine is there, amid a stand of like-minded wood and steel. I hang my head and pray for the thought to be taken from me. When I look again upon my father I see that I have not been answered.

I take the rifle from the cabinet and reach for one of the loose shells strewn on a shelf. I drop the bullet in the chamber and ease the bolt shut. Seeing that my father still sleeps, I allow myself to breath. From a spot behind his chair I draw the rifle to my shoulder and bear down on his skull. In the darkness it's impossible to make out the sights, but at this distance such things are unnecessary. I whisper what I think of him. *Son of a bitch,* I hear myself hiss. *You son of a bitch.*

I see him face down, nuzzling the soft knap of the carpet—his large, limp carcass wheel-barrowed to the smoldering fire-pit—a stick poked through the empty eye socket and his skull lifted from the ash for inspection.

There is the dull click of my finger finding the safety, but that same finger will not enter the ring of the trigger guard. I don't have the feeling for it. I let the gun down and delicately rest my hand on my father's head. His moist, pomaded hair clings to my palm. Still he does not move. I know full-well that once my mother sent word, once the family arrived, my own corpse would quickly find its way to the coal bed. I try to slow my breathing. I drag my sweating palms up and down on the thighs of my pants. I wonder if my father felt this fear, the day he came for me in the shed.

I make my way before him. His chin hangs, his mouth slightly open. His shirt crinkles and settles with the movement of his chest. I want to be the bullet that makes its way into his brain. I want to splay his skull and knead the insides to better know them. But this man, I could not stand him dead. Choking on my breath, I fall to my knees.

My hand falls upon his bare foot—it feels cold against the damp heat of my palm. In this arrangement I see what must be done. I ease up high on my knees and draw the barrel of the carbine down on the back of my hand. The cold circle of the muzzle settles in the center of my hand, between the bones. I slide my hand a touch higher on his foot so as not to shoot one of his toes off. I look up and flinch at the flicker of light in my father's eyes. My body stalls. He looks to the ceiling and whispers something. His eyes fall again upon me and he speaks,

"We have been blind."

My breathing shudders. "I'm sorry," I say.

"No," he says, shaking his head. "I pointed to their pride. All the while believing virtue mine to bestow. I am the one to apologize."

I snuffle a bit. I fall back to my heels and let the gun slide from my shoulder.

In a flash my father lurches forward and clutches a fistful of my hair. I am startled as he draws me back to my knees.

"Don't be afraid," he says. "Don't let doubt lead us any further."

Our eyes meet. His fist releases its grip. His warm, heavy palm pats my hair back into place. I slowly allow my face to smile. My chest fills with something when he returns the gesture.

"Thank you," I say.

He exhales and I hear the arms of the recliner strain under the strength of his clenched hands. He nods and I look down at my target.

Our Time is Up

CRIS MAZZA

1987

The word, that year, was *co-dependant*. Barb was in a co-dependency group. Too young for a *midlife crisis* (that, believe it or not, was from 1965), but was exactly where she should be to begin probing the concerns of *adult children* (1983). *Yuppies*, identified in 1984, had already discovered if their families had been *dysfunctional* (1981), and were ready become *empowered* (1986) but first would need co-dependency therapy. They wouldn't *reinvent themselves* until 1989 and couldn't find their *inner children* until 1990.

Barb was only half-listening when the counselor began her opening speech at the first meeting. Besides Barb there were three other women. Somehow Barb had already learned: MaryPat was a waitress who used to be something else. Gloria was loud and flamboyant, newly di-

> *... you may deplore the behavior—it may hurt you, terrify you, drive a wedge between you and your spouse or child or parent; it might make you feel hopeless, helpless, frustrated, angry. But are YOU helping to keep, to maintain the trouble in your re-*

vorced, and Barb didn't know what she did. Belinda did something in an insurance office and had two pet rabbits and a husband who traveled a lot. The counselor had been seeing at least two of the other women alone, and had recently decided to have group sessions. So when Barb had been calling the numbers listed in the phonebook under counseling, this was the first one who'd said she had an opening in a new group for women she was starting. How was Barb to know the counselor held ses-

lationship? Are you addicted to the addiction? If you do anything to assist the addicted person to get through his or her day, you are co-dependent, and you are EN-ABLING. You're assisting them to continue their dependence—that is, allowing the condition to-continue and even to get worse. If you grew up this way, being co-dependent to an addictive parent, your dysfunctional family experience trained you that this is the only way to subsist, to co-exist in a relationship, and so you will likely be co-dependent in your adult relationships. It is only by breaking the cycle that you can experience a healthy, supportive relationship.

sions in a small bedroom converted into an office in her apartment in one of those old neighborhoods near the park where a jet had crashed a few years after they'd moved here, the type of place where everyone was a vegetarian and still wore their graying hair long and parted in the middle and didn't shave their legs and let their horny toenails show through leather sandals while they were holding group counseling. And it took over an hour to get to San Diego from their condo in Del Mar, so she'd had to miss her afternoon aerobics class and sit in Friday afternoon gridlock to get here. Who had group therapy on Friday?

After she had found the group, but before the first meeting, last Saturday morning, Bobby found her where she was reading on the pool deck. He was holding a folded newspaper and said, "I know you like dance movies. There's a new one, let's go see it."

She'd looked at him and almost said, "Don't try so hard. It hurts." But she went to the movie with him. It was Dirty Dancing. Near the beginning, Bobby leaned over and whispered, "They can't be serious, a character named *Baby*?" Afterwards he said the movie had reached new levels of cheesiness.

> There are other expressions of co-dependency besides enabling an addict. Much of it stems from low self-esteem, so you may have been abused or neglected as a child. You may be someone who will decide what to do based on how much it will please others.

Barb bought the soundtrack, the next day after work. Bought it on LP even though they were trying to switch, but the album had a larger picture of Patrick Swayze than the cassette or CD. Before Bobby came home, she made a cassette and put it in her car, unmarked. Bobby would never notice the album, slipped in between Flashdance and Fame, to the right of WHAM (Take Me Out Before you Go-Go). Tuesday afternoon, she asked the aerobics coach to use her Dirty Dancing tape, even though she knew exercise tapes had to be custom mixed so all the tunes were the proper speed: warm-up, build-up, aerobic peak and maintenance, through warm-down. Dirty Dancing had all different tempos, and they came in movie-plot order. Growing up, learning about sex, falling in love, then profoundly changing someone's life didn't necessarily happen in the same progression as heart rate during aerobics class. So she listened to the cassette going to and from work, Wednesday and Thursday, and going to work this morning, and on her way to group an hour ago.

Barb was on a sofa with compressed cushions, the brown

> You may only be able to feel good about yourself when you are helping someone or listening to a friend describe her problems. Then if you're in a situation where you need help, you may turn away from help, feel uncomfortable receiving that kind of attention. You may appear to all the world as a competent adult, but you're so focused on

plaid fabric pilled and scratchy. Belinda was beside her. The counselor was in a scratched dining-table chair to Barb's left. This put the counselor's *what others need and how you can please them, you know very little about how to direct your own life.*

bare toes closest to Barb. Gloria sat in another dining chair facing the counselor, and MaryPat, on a vinyl avocado green ottoman, faced the sofa.

Barb's husband didn't drink, smoke, gamble, or do drugs. Both sets of their parents were still married, hadn't ever beat them or their siblings, hadn't tried to have sex with them, hadn't neglected them at Christmas or birthdays, came to their school plays and band concerts, likewise didn't drink, smoke, gamble, over-eat or do drugs. Couldn't you have all that and still be unhappy?

Now Gloria was talking: *...to be for the first time only responsible for mySELF, and I'll tell you, it's so empowering. I even enjoy doing my laundry and cooking my dinner. I'm the one deciding when to go to bed and when to get up—at least on weekends. Weekdays I still have to be at work at 7 a.m. But I'm going to start applying this whole concept to my boss too. I've enabled him to be disorganized because he knows I'll keep track of everything, I'll never let him miss an appointment or lose a file or forget to pay a bill. I guess it's made me*

Barb was deciding what she should say when it was her turn. How much would be enough? Start where she and Bobby moved here from Terre Haute in 1976 the day after he graduated from ISU with his engineering degree? Neither of them even had a job, and within four days of arriving, amid the unemployment of the late 70s, she'd started

feel important that he needs me so much, so now I understand: I'm co-dependent to the scatterbrained contractor, and believe me, he is addicted to his own organizational incompetence because it makes him feel more important. HE does the creative or important thinking and decision making, I'm just the dull administrative

making appointments and checking patients in at Dr. Easly's old office in Santee. Bobby found his job a few weeks later, a civilian company with contracts from the Navy, but he'd moved from that job, and had moved several other times before finding the one he stayed with, designing recycling machines for a local company that sells them to municipalities and waste management companies (commonly called dumps) all over the world... But that was really getting off the point, even though Bobby's cutting-edge work would make the rest of these women's husbands or exes look like redneck meatballs, but that wasn't really the point either.

Someone else had started talking ...

assistant who can only think in daily details. But as soon as I stop enabling, I'll be out of that cycle and can empower myself with other kinds of value. That book just absolutely changed my LIFE. Like when my ex tried to come in the house last night, claiming he needed to get his tools and it was part of the agreement—I wouldn't let him in. I'd changed the locks. When I'd made this so-called agreement, I was still being co-dependent, allowing him to bully me into getting his own way just because it was easier than fighting. So in my mind it's invalid.

It was MaryPat: "But ... if you didn't make appointments and file...I mean, isn't that your job?"

"It doesn't have to be who I *am*."

"So I serve drinks to drunks. It isn't who I am, and it doesn't mean they've forced me to be a waitress. I chose to be a waitress because I make a hell of a lot more money than when I was a junior high band teacher."

"MaryPat," said the counselor, drawing her sandaled toes back underneath her dining-table chair, "is there some subtext you'd like to share?"

Yeah, we were both music majors, and we both wanted to be band directors, but all along, now that I look back, they were aiming me toward junior high while it was always understood he would have a high school. And that's exactly how it turned out. Bruce was Mr. Important field-tournament-band-director, bussing to Los Angeles, to Phoenix, to Santa Barbara for tournaments with his entourage of equipment trucks and band parents wearing some kind of their own uniform, horning in on their kids' high school life, coming home with trophies, blah, blah blah, while there I was teaching Mary's Little Lamb *to 11 year olds spitting into trumpets for half the pay. Well, not* HALF, *but not even three-quarters. So I quit and went back to waitressing and now I make more than him, but obviously I work nights and we barely ever see each other, especially weekends when his buses have to leave the school at around*

Barb is trying to listen to this one, but she honestly can't imagine how anyone could care if their husband's dumb band got some trophy and yours didn't. Bobby makes model cars and little radio-controlled airplanes and sometimes comes home from his weekend shindigs with a plaque or a ribbon, and Barb didn't start complaining it was a chauvinistic plot. She could give a flying flip about his little cars and airplanes, really, even though he tries to show her the minutest details on them (sometimes she has to just pretend to be seeing what he's talking about).

5 a.m. to get to whatever tournament they're doing. And when he gets home, he expects me to have waited all day just to find out how well his band did. If I don't gasp with enough awe, he gets cranky, and there's another evening we barely speak.

"So you're enabling him to out-do you by quitting and letting him be the star," Gloria said, shifting her butt and re-crossing her legs as she spoke. Like Barb, she hadn't changed from her skirt and pumps before coming to the group, but Gloria's nylons looked too glossy. "You're actually addicted to being second chair."

"I just said I make more money than he does. I just can't always be saying oh-you're-such-a-wonderful-high-school-band-director-honey with any real enthusiasm."

"Maybe you're greeting him with other kinds of you-messages," the counselor said. "You should concentrate on using only I-messages. Do you know what that means?"

MaryPat shook her head, so the counselor started explaining. Barb felt like she was falling into the crushed sofa, like her butt suddenly weighed twice as much. Which is often what happened when she missed aerobics. Friday there was jazzercise after aerobics, and Bobby always stayed at his office Friday afternoon, having a beer with his partner and waiting for the rush-to-weekend traffic to pass. There was never any reason to believe it wasn't what he was doing. Until he surprised her a few months ago. But she's not going to start

You-messages can easily be, and often are, accusatory, even hostile. Why did you do that? You're making me feel worthless. You were late. You're being insensitive. You're not being fair. You're spending too much. You're the one who thought we should buy this. Most people will get defensive when receiving you-messages, and then a useful communication will be impossible. Try I-messages instead: I feel sad that this is happening. I'm trying to understand why you're upset. I'm sorry you feel that way. I'm worried about our money. I-messages invite the other person to communicate, rather than shut the doors to communication.

there. Is it important to say that they met while Bobby was in college, but she wasn't a student, she just happened to grow up in Terre Haute? After she graduated from high school, she started right away as a key punch operator at Fieldcrest Industries. She'd been working there three years when she met Bobby, and went on working there after they (secretly) moved in together before they got married. She'd cried the night of their wedding, but not the tears-of-joy weeping girls did in the novels Barb read; she'd never done that kind of crying and didn't know why—what was wrong with her? That night Bobby had asked her why she was crying and all she could think of was, "I just thought never I'd get married." Was that an I-message? They were all practicing their I-messages.

"I feel I'm ready to participate more in the business," Gloria said to her contractor boss.

As if any contractor was going to ask his secretary for construction advice—like how many nails he would need, how much cement?

"I'm sad that my plans to be a band director got wrecked," MaryPat said to her band directing husband, "and yours didn't."

"Should he apologize for that?" the counselor asked.

"Okay—I'm sorry that you think I should be happy that my plans got wrecked and yours didn't?"

"You don't *sound* like you *chose* to be a waitress," Gloria said.

What a ball-bender, that's what Bobby called women like that one.

"That's a you-message," MaryPat returned. "Besides, a waitress is almost a self-sufficient private contractor. It's one of the few things women have if they want to be independent."

Another would be prostitution.

"I don't like spending so much time without you," Belinda said to her traveling husband.

"Have you said that to him?" the counselor asked.

"Yes. I think so. I don't know."

"Or did you say, 'why do you have to leave me alone so often?'" Gloria asked.

Who's the counselor here anyway?

"Maybe. I don't know."

"What does he say?" the counselor asked.

How about Get a life?

"If I say anything about it, he gets real quiet and goes to watch TV or sits in his study. He says traveling is what makes him like his job so much. He bought me the rabbits so I wouldn't be alone."

"Long-eared rats are no substitute for a husband," Gloria said.

"Why not a dog?" MaryPat asked.

"They don't allow dogs in our apartment."

"I'm going to get a dog," MaryPat said. "I think I want a dog with papers. I want to show it."

Are there enough I-messages in that one? "I think that would be good for you," the counselor approved. She turned toward Barb. "We haven't heard from you yet, Barb."

While Barb is talking in group therapy, Bobby is still in his office at the recycling machine company, with Carl, the other engineer, having a few beers and waiting for Friday rush traffic to dissipate. It's September, so they talk about football. The Chargers haven't lost enough games to be out of contention yet, but the baseball team was a lost cause months ago and isn't worth an exchange of two sentences, except to bemoan how the Chargers have to play with a dirt infield outline on their football field grass until the baseball season mercifully ends at the end of the month.

One Friday Carl had brought Wild Turkey and they'd done shots, and Carl had the brilliant idea to call a guy he knew in the manufacturing unit who knew how to contact a girl who would come over and give blow jobs for fifty bucks. They did, one at a time, in the engineering office, while the other sat just outside. Bobby had never had a blow job before, but he didn't admit it to Carl. Barb said asking a woman to do it was demeaning to her, not just because you're asking her to put his body's waste-emptying conduit into her mouth, but because he could experience the whole thing without once touching her, and, in fact, it was like he could be alone, watching TV while he got it. He didn't know how it was much different than the hand jobs she gave him to "take care of him" when he was horny and she wanted to go to sleep. She didn't use the word *conduit*; she probably made up some medical-sounding word, which she was prone to do at parties when she made pronouncements about vitamins or nutrition and he saw people exchange glances. He took a long time to come because he did feel weird about it, coming in the girl's mouth, but she wasn't being paid by the hour, and Carl didn't say anything about how long he'd sat outside the door; he'd already had his turn.

About a month later, Carl brought up calling the girl again, and he still sometimes suggested it, maybe once a month, but Bobby always said, "We don't have anything stronger than beer," and Carl let it drop. Bobby had already told Carl about his worry that something was going on between Barb and someone at the doctor's office she worked at—not the doctor, but someone like a doctor. Barb had said it would take too long to explain what a PA was, more than a nurse and less than a doctor, she'd said. As though he was some geek with his head up his butt.

Since they do this almost every Friday, Bobby doesn't bother to tell Carl that Barb is at her first group therapy meeting. It had been her idea to go. While she'd been deciding, and vacillating, he'd tried to be encouraging toward whichever way she chose, individual, group, or none at all. She'd been dramatically listless—at least when he saw her, at home—since that night three months ago. He didn't know what she was like at work. He couldn't imagine how she would describe that night, or what else she might be saying tonight, like what was going on inside the house in Tierrasanta that he had waited outside for over an hour. After Barb had come out of the house and walked past him—giving him only a startled look, and maybe even saying "hi," (*hi*? as though they were meeting on a campus between classes?)—he'd gone straight to his office, this office. Another time that he sat in his office, long after working hours were over, except without Carl, and without a girl giving him a blowjob. He'd already had Kathy's phone number in his wallet. He'd had it for a few weeks, since he'd called information in Terre Haute. He sat for a while before calling. Kept hearing Barb saying "hi," but not really sure if she'd really said it, or maybe *he* said it. Maybe he was the one who said it, from the darkness under the tree he stood beside, and that's when he'd seen her surprised look.

While everybody looked at her, listening, Barb said: *I don't know how it happened ... it just ... I don't know ... happened. I met someone who ... listened to me, thought I was funny and ... I don't know ... smart ... He understood the things that worry and bother me, and ... talked to me about what worried and bothered him. With him, I felt so ... I don't know ... more myself ... like I was myself for the first time in my life. And I ... But I ... couldn't be with him because ... I don't know ... he was engaged ... He'd been engaged for so long, but wasn't married ... He'd been married before, but ... I don't know ... that doesn't matter ... He lived alone. Lives alone. He ... Sometimes I ... need to talk to someone ... about things ... Just things that ... I don't know. It had been three months. One ... or two days a week... I went home with him, instead of to my aerobics class. I needed it. It was something I ... I don't know ... had never had. Then ... it wasn't right for him, for Bobby to ... follow me like I was a criminal ... and spy on me ... I don't check on him when he stays after work and drinks with his buddy. He told me what they do and I believe him. I don't remember what I told him ... I told him something ... he should've believed me ... I might have said I need*

> She wasn't looking at them anymore. She picked at a little loose ball of nylon on her knee.

to do something ... that I needed to ... It was something I needed

She wasn't going to tell them what she and Hal did. It would desecrate it to reduce it to words. They were the most beautiful, sheer, breathtaking, alive moments of her life—that's what drug addicts probably said, but she didn't need drugs—but she wasn't going to give it away by trying to explain.

... to do. To do for me. If I didn't ... take care of myself ... like my aerobics ... I ... I don't know ... But anyway, he followed me ... I don't know how long he was there. He was standing outside when I left. Just standing there in the dark like a secret agent. When I told Hal, the next day at work, he ... later he said we needed to ... stop. The shit hit the fan for him too, he said. Just like that. His fiancé was getting uncomfortable and asking questions, he said. It was ... so easy for him ... to say it. So easy for both of them to just ... I don't know ... tell me I can't have ... what I need.

From where he stood in the dark outside the PA's house in Tierrasanta, Bobby had gone directly to his office in Chula Vista, which was the opposite direction from the condo in Del Mar. But while he'd stood outside that house in the dark, on the parkway beside the sidewalk, under a tree that rained some kind of pollen or seed shit he later found in his hair, what had he thought about? Sometimes Barb asked what he was thinking, and she didn't like his answer: that he was hungry, that his football team was lousy, that he was too tired to get up. That night, if she'd asked instead of walking past, he could've said he was thinking about how they periodically found old World War II munitions buried in backyards or empty lots in Tierrasanta, because during the War it had been an empty Navy testing ground, far from any populated areas, and now it was in the middle of a city, a whole community with a name that meant Sacred Ground. Bobby had learned some Spanish before moving to California because he'd heard it could help you get a job. He'd learned from tapes, listening to them over and over during the drive from Indiana—he drove the U-Haul and Barb the Datsun—and also had practiced by looking up in a dictionary the English translation for all the town and community names. *Of the Sea ... Hidden Valley ... View of the Ocean ... View of the Plateau ... Beautiful View ...* and just plain *Beautiful.* So he'd gotten curious and wondered what Terre Haute meant. It was French and meant High Ground. So, standing there in Tierrasanta, he'd thought about coming from high ground to sacred ground.

He made the call from his office in Chula Vista, which he hadn't been able to translate with his little dictionary. A view of something. His dictionary, still on his desk, said Chulo meant pimp. That was weird. He hadn't thought about that for a long time, not even when they'd called the girl to give blow jobs. She had been a Mexican girl, and that had troubled him. He'd become the Ugly American. With Kathy, he had only kissed her and touched her large breasts through her sweater or blouse, and yet it had been far more exciting than his first blow job.

It was almost nine o'clock in Terre Haute. It would be 10 o'clock if it weren't daylight savings time, but Indiana didn't use daylight savings.

Kathy answered. A simple, uncomplicated "Hello?"

"Hi," he'd said. "It's ... Bobby."

"Pardon me?"

"Bobby. Bobby Winston."

"I'm sorry?"

"Remember ... from high school?"

"Oh."

"I'm calling from California."

"Oh ...?"

"I moved here after college. I guess I haven't talked to you since before that. I don't remember the last time we ..."

"Oh, *Bobby*."

"Yeah, it's me." His voice almost a whisper.

"I'm sorry, I guess I haven't thought about high school for so long."

"Yeah, me neither. I got married and graduated and moved ... Or graduated and married and moved ... I don't remember. So, how are you? You didn't get married? I mean, your number is listed with your last name, I remembered it—"

"I'm divorced."

"That's good." He swallowed, blinked hard. "I mean, maybe you can tell me, what *that's* like ... I mean ... it's hard, being married. Isn't it?"

"Why are you calling, Bobby?"

"No reason. Just to say Hi. I just thought I'd see what you were up to."

"Why? That was high school. I've been married, divorced. Then I made a clean break from that part of my life. I'm born again. I can't be taking calls from another woman's husband."

"I didn't mean ..."

"Goodbye, Bobby."

There was a moment of silence. Barb wiped her last tears. She was holding a Kleenex she doesn't remember taking from a box beside her. She looked up, and then they started:

Oh, wow, been-there-done-THAT ... I've been the one picking up the phone and hearing it disconnect. I've been the one wondering why it takes so long for him to drive home from his job 15 minutes away. I've been the one finding the Virginia Slims cigarette box in his car, the one wondering why his court shoes are still at home but

Not looking at them anymore, again. The loose ball of nylon was now the start of a run from her knee to her thigh. Not sure she's still breathing.

he said he was playing basketball after work, the one crying myself to sleep because of that bastard and his current floozy. Who's the co-dependent here? Maybe your husband needs co-dependency therapy, he's the one not divorcing you after finding out you're cheating. HE'S enabling YOU ...

How could I expect you to understand. Rabbits really are the perfect pet for you.

I would never do that. I could just never do that. Randy's away from home so much, but ... I could just never do that. That's ... just something I could never do.

Are you sure you're in the right group? I mean, maybe it is my fault I gave up, and it galls me that Bruce's band is winning all the time, but ... to go behind his back,

You're right, this is obviously the wrong place, the wrong group, the wrong... oh my god, why did I come here?.

to have an AFFAIR? That wouldn't be my answer. And believe me, it wouldn't be difficult to find some-one, in my line of work. But that's just tacky. It sounds like a soap opera. It sounds like the drama is what you're after. Like coming here and crying is part of the whole deal, and you like it as much as the sneaking around and cheating. Is that it? Didn't you ever ask yourself IS THIS ALL THERE IS? You yup-pies—isn't that a Beemer you drove here in?—what's the UP for you anyway, what do you WANT?

Barb, maybe we need to hear about your feelings in a different way. What did you want from the group when you shared?

"I don't know."

She could hear herself answer-ing, and the questions came from everywhere, the know-it-all, the surly ex-band-direc-tor, the rabbit girl, the hairy-legged counselor. She didn't remember the kleenex box

No, I think MaryPat meant what were her upwardly-mobile goals?

"To be ... To not have to work someday. For my hus-band to ..."

moving to her lap. She kept hearing herself answering, but she was thinking about getting into that BMW which seemed to have made the band director so angry—or even more angry—and start driving and keep driving, all the way back to Terre Haute. She'd had such a cute studio apartment there, near the campus, near the football stadium—she should tell MaryPat how she could hear the drums and knew when it was halftime—until she'd meet Bobby, a student living across the hall with 2 other guys, then somehow her cute apartment was gone and she was living beside the train tracks with Bobby, in a building filled with college kids, a place she'd been glad to leave for the adventure of moving to California. And now …

What—did you want to have children and stay at home and have no financial independence? Why didn't you go to college?

"I don't know."

Why don't you have children?

"I don't know."

You say that a lot.

Did you ever ask your husband about it, Barb?

"I don't know. I think so."

What did he say?

"That I never said anything so he never said anything."

Didn't he want children?

"I don't know. We liked the way things were."

Then why are you unhappy now?

And why did you cheat with someone else's man?

"I don't know. It just happened."

That's what addicts say, they don't take responsibility. You could've just-said-no.

What *had* she wanted, ever, once upon a time or even a year ago? And why had she moved here? Because Bobby had been preparing for four years and had decided, before he met her, to get out of Indiana and go somewhere where the things an engineer did could matter to the world. The day after graduation, that's what

Is there an AA for soap opera addicts who try to live like they're in one?

I read they have CoDA organizations, a 12-step group, I guess we're not a big enough group for that kind of thing?

12-steps are religiously based,

he did, and by then she was beside him, packing a U-haul long into the night. That had been ten years ago. Did she ever wonder, that night, if she were single, would she have chosen this? But what *else* would she have done? Before she met Bobby, what did she think she'd be doing in a year, in ten years? Had she ever given it a single thought, or was the naive pleasure of paying her own rent and arranging her own things in her single room and buying her own bag of groceries once a week too much of a giddy drug? But once here, she'd become comfortable, immediately, with things she enjoyed: walking on the beach, especially in the winter when the threat of burning into blistered, peeling red paint was past; or her jazzercise classes with other women who tore the neckbands out of their sweatshirts; or the condo's pool where she read a book every week and could casually say to people at the office, I *read a book a week*, even though Bobby called them *rescue-me-fuck-me* books. Hal liked her to read to him.

but here we can support each—

Coda is a music term, a passage at the end of a piece or movement that brings it to a close.

It's for Co-dependants Anonymous. So let's bring our co-dependency to a close. Your band can play a symphony when my boss realizes I'm not a doormat.

I don't have a band. Doing your job isn't being a doormat.

Not getting credit for it is. Isn't that why you quit?

I changed jobs.

Tomato tow-ma-to. You should at least tell him the real reason you did it. You should get the book, really, it changed my life.

Girls, I think our time is up.

Girl, as a pejorative, never earned the horrific level of *boy*. In fact, just the opposite. It even became *girl power* (1986), while *boy*, racist undertones notwithstanding, at best was limited to its *toy* rhyme-ability or connotation, as in *game boy* (1989). An adult male did not want to be a *boy*, but could be a *New Man* (1982) which, near the end of the decade had disintegrated into a wimp or *wuss* (1984). Being a *girl* was better than being *wimmin* (1983, a spelling to remove the word *man*). While *girl* hadn't yet become *grrl* (1994, but not an attempt to remove the *I* from *girl*) the pretty, gentle word may have helped women feel younger, even pleasantly vulnerable. Or less alone, as in *girlfriend*.

Barb never went back to the group, and she quit her job at Dr. Easly's office, even though she might have become office manager someday. Bobby either didn't notice or didn't comment, until she told him she found a better job at a hospital doing outpatient and emergency room billing. He said, "That's good, you'll probably get some additional computer training." Doctors never came into the office where her desk was, where she kept a picture of Bobby beside her telephone, and a magazine cover of Patrick Swayze in her drawer.

One day, when Bobby didn't want to figure out how to use the coffee maker, he was going to boil some water for instant coffee and found a video tape hidden in a pot in the cupboard. Of course he played it and found an interview with Patrick Swayze on Entertainment Tonight.

Meanwhile, there were always new words. For example: The *virtual reality* (1987) of rush hour traffic is that *road rage* (1988) is like a dance movie *from hell* (1987) where you can't tell *moshing* (1987) from *wilding* (1989).

Bobby came home one day and went directly to where Barb was reading on the pool deck and told her he was moving out. Barb cried for what seemed like three days straight. There was no one to ask her why. She had to pretend Bobby was dead, like Patrick Swayze in *Ghost*, and had told her he'd love and protect her forever, and was hovering near her every moment, looking over her. When Bobby started seeing someone, Barb told him she was dating a doctor named Patrick. But eventually Patrick had to leave to open a clinic in … Paris. Of all places, Paris needed a clinic with a handsome American doctor named Patrick. Barb could've started a Patrick-Swayze-anonymous group—PSA, like the airline that had fallen from the sky, just a few years after they'd moved here from Terre Haute, and exploded not far from where the fading hippy counselor held co-dependency therapy.

❧ *The Taste of Penny* ❧

JEFF PARKER

It was as simple as this: Brotherman's had a little problem with its local competitors, The Two Men And A Truck crew. The Two Men And A Truck crew are former cops.

Now Steve is standing here on the side of the road with a current cop, and his finger, a part of himself which he loathes, pokes into the meaty ball in the corner of his eye. At first he's shocked to see the thing there and thinks it's someone else's. But he recognizes the sad condition of his own digit in the bright glare of the street light, as it misses his nose completely.

This sad condition was a constant source of embarrassment. Just the other day two girls, strangers in some waiting area, suggested that he get a manicure.

"I don't even know you," he said to them.

"They're really bad," one of them said, "your nails."

"But do you think it's your place to tell someone something like that?"

"They're disgusting," said the other one.

Steve had always known they were disgusting fingers, spindly and crooked from breaking them as a kid. He couldn't recall ever having a full nail. He bit them down to nothing—a habit he'd recently been trying to break, going around with hot sauce coating them, reeking of cayenne and vinegar.

The surprise of that one appearing where it isn't supposed to and sticking him in the eye makes him lose track of the penny hidden under his tongue, and swallow it.

Much of the pull-over he doesn't remember, only the highlights…sliding a penny from the ashtray and dropping it on his tongue…scratching his eyeball so bad the penny slides right down his throat…

Immediately Steve begins—maybe this isn't the right word—*sensing* the penny in his stomach. He experiences two distinct sensations: the pressure of his palm on the back of his eyelid, and the discomfort of the penny inside him, a presence. If he moves the hand, pain lights up in his eye.

Steve and the cop stand there a few silent minutes looking at each other on the side of the road. The cop looks at Steve, and Steve looks at the cop. He blinks his one eye. He keeps the other eye covered with his palm, pointing his fingers outward like lashes. He doesn't even want to touch himself with them. Not in the eye, not on his dick. He wants to keep his fingers away from himself.

Steve doesn't know what to do with his other arm so it hangs limp at his side. He does not have his swerve on.

"So it's like that is it?" the cop says.

"Like how?"

There is no response.

"I think I really did something to my eye," Steve says. "I can't seem to take my hand away from it."

"You know what I think, sir?" the cop says.

"I don't know."

"I'll tell you. I think your eye's not hurt. I think you're trying to get out of something." The cop believes Steve to be bullshitting. He believes him to be drunk as well.

"Oh it's hurt. It's definitely hurt."

"And I don't suppose you could pass anymore tests then huh?"

"It'd be difficult. I am happy to try. It'd not be easy. Not one bit. However I am cooperative. I will do what you ask. I am being cooperative."

The cop walks Steve to the squad car. He jostles him some, testing his swerve for himself. Steve is steadfast. Nevermind he missed his nose. Steve is the best drunk driver you'll meet. He'd been pulled over not because of the seatbelt either. No one can see that you're not wearing your seatbelt. Everyone knows that is some bullshit excuse law. He'd been pulled for his magnetic signs, and he should have known better.

He'd won them off a sign painter, in a drinking contest, and he could peel them off at anytime. But they were fantastic white magnetic signs, and Steve was proud of them. They announced in the way the constant flyering at the grocery store didn't that he ran a real business. In beveled yellow letters, a yellow so fantastic you could almost call it neon, "Brotherman's Hauling".

But this is Steve's perspective. He is actually a piss-poor drunk driver. He has been for years.

…the cop shoving him into the backseat…looking at him again, crouched down in front of his face, a distinct fishy scent on his breath…

"Remove your mitt from your facial area." Steve does and brushes the cop's cheek. "Jesus Christ," the cop says. "Watch those things."

"Apology," Steve says.

"Now open it."

Steve tries, but he can only manage a tight squint. Everything is blurred, and the effort it takes to open that one forces the other one closed.

"How many fingers am I holding?" the cop says.

"I have no idea." Which he does not. He sees refracted light, lots of refracted light, and shapes.

"Well don't lay down back there," the cop says.

"Why would I lay down?"

"Some people lay down." The cop shuts the door behind him then climbs in the front and radios for an ambulance. With the dispatcher, he refers to Steve as "some numb nuts who seems to have poked his own eye during the drunk test."

Instinctively, Steve gnaws the thumbnail of his spare hand. He need not even, as he usually does, remind himself of the protein in fingernail.

When the cop opens the door again, he has a little gadget with a tube coming off it. "While we're waiting, you don't need either one of your eyes to blow into this."

…blowing into the breathalyzer…the readout on the breath-alyzer mercifully holding at point zero seven nine, just one one-thousandth from some jail, some losing some license, some losing some business…the EMTs installing a patch over the eye…driving away angry and horny and extremely hungry for Taco Bell…

Brotherman's little problem was—you know, there'd been no problem when the Two Men stuck to moving. But maybe the moving business wasn't too hot or something. Just last week they stumbled across a flyer at the PriceChopper that read, "Two Men And A Truck: Moving, AND NOW HAULING TOO." Technically, yes, movers and haulers both haul things. They also both move them. But to Steve's mind the distinction was crystal: Things that people want or care about are moved. Things that people don't want or care about are hauled.

In some towns the Two Men And A Truck company is a franchise, the kind of place that hires buff frat boys and deducts FICA. This Two Men And A Truck was just that, two men and a pick-up, just like Steve and Jeremy, the F-150, and Brotherman's Hauling. Steve and Jeremy might even have welcomed their expansion, a little competition, had those fuckers not tacked their flyers up directly over the Brotherman's flyers.

Exactly one week before the pull-over, Steve took one of the tear-off phone numbers from the Two Men flyer. He then called with a fake hauling job. "It's a little drive out of town," he said. "But the payoff is worth it."

"We have a few moving gigs scheduled," one of the Two Men said. "If it's that big we can cancel them."

Steve described the job to him. The job he pitched was a point-by-point description of the first hauling job Brotherman's had ever done, transporting five hundred eighty-gallon drums, the kind bums make fires in, to the barrel refurbishing plant. The plant's drivers had gone on a strike. It had required precision stacking, four-inch truck cargo straps, and multiple trips to haul it all in the F-150. But it had paid extremely well. That one job funded the whole business. It bought Brotherman's computer and the mobile. Steve described the job to the one man, who sounded very eager. Steve gave him a fake address of a drum processing facility on the Old Highway. He gave him a fake phone number too.

So when the mobile buzzed later that evening he didn't think anything much of it. Steve's plans have simple flaws. It was actually the two men of Two Men on at the same time.

"You cost us a day, pussboy," said one of them, Steve thought the same one he talked to earlier.

"A day," said the other one.

"That's brotherman to you," Steve said. "You have conference call or something? How do you get that?"

"Yeah, we got conference call," said the first one. "And you got a genuine problem."

"What are they saying?" Jeremy said.

"They say we've got a problem," Steve said.

"Talking to your pussy, dick?" one of the two men said. Steve couldn't tell them apart anymore.

"They ask if I'm talking to my pussy," Steve said.

"Tell them your pussy takes umbrage at their comment," Jeremy said.

"Takes what?"

"You guys need to watch your backs. This ain't cool. We let you run your little show around here long enough. Now there may be some action."

"An equal and opposite reaction?" Steve said in the voice of a black man imitating a white man.

"*Um-bridge,*" Jeremy said.

"Payback action," the two men said.

"My pussy takes umbrage at your comment," Steve said.

"Umbrage *to* your comment," one of them said, and they hung up.

Steve regretted making the phony call.

"Well?" Jeremy said.

"They corrected you."

"Corrected what?"

"They said it's umbrage to your comment."

"Bullshit," Jeremy said. "Bullfuckingshit."

Steve is hyperaware of his shit as it moves through him. He searches the bowl. He probes with a wire coat hanger, but there's no penny. He feels it still, somewhere within him, a point of pressure there above his stomach, a little insignificant weight.

He removes two bowls of hot sauce from the fridge and soaks his fingers for ten minutes like he's seen women in manicure shops soaking their fingers. When time is up, he drip-dries over the bowls. The tips turn a crusty orange. They sting and tighten.

Because the floors in Steve's apartment are paper-thin, the Red-haired Girl down stairs can hear him masturbating at his computer. Except today he's as silent as possible. He uses a poly-ethylene glove coated in cocoa butter on his right hand and runs the mouse with his left.

He knows she can hear him because yesterday, before he started drinking, the Red-haired Girl had a little talk with him during which he pretty much got the picture. She knocked on his door while he had the news on. She told him the news was too loud.

"It's the news," he said. "How can the news be loud?"

"I can hear everything that goes on up here," she said. "*Everything.*" This being her subtle hint that he might want to check the volume at which he engages Internet porn. He understood that she issued her complaint intentionally during an innocent moderate-volume news moment so as to get her point across when he was not in the middle of the activity she really wanted to put a stop to. She was smart, he figured. Of course he knew how troubling it was to be able to hear something like that. He could hear the guy above him jerking off to Internet porn too. Some faggots might find the guy above you jerking off at the same time as you exciting. It bugged Steve though. And because he could never hear the Red-haired Girl down stairs doing anything, he knew the guy upstairs could not hear him. Sound moves downward, he thought.

So when he breaks for attempting to expel the penny again, he hears the guy upstairs watching *The Price Is Right* at a nor-mal volume—normal in this building means, in the quiet of his apartment one floor removed, he hears the sound of Bob Barker's voice over his own bathroom fan.

Steve goes upstairs and knocks on the door. He keeps his hands in his pockets.

"Hey neighbor," the guy says. "Why the eye patch?" They have never spoken before.

"Work injury," Steve says.

"Workman's comp. That's my secret." He grabs his thigh and says, "Oh my leg!" He hops around in his foyer. "If you know what I mean."

Steve delivers the exact same lines the Red-haired Girl used on him, and the guy upstairs responds at first pretty much as he had.

"Loudness is a subjective thing," the guy says.

"I can hear everything that goes on up here," Steve says. "*Everything*." He tries to approximate the Red-haired Girl's expression. And he thinks the guy upstairs gets it, just as he had gotten it. Unlike Steve though, he pushes.

"Give me an example?" the guy says.

"Oh, I can, you know, just about everything. You walking around. Opening the refrigerator, listening to music, the boob tube."

"Like what? What was I watching at two a.m. this morning?"

"I don't actually log," Steve says.

"Sure you're not just an asshole?" the guy asks, sincerely Steve thinks.

"No, look, it's just that these apartments suck. I can hear everything all right."

"To travel, sound requires a medium of transmission. For instance, solid, liquid, or air. I suppose I could convert my apartment into a vacuum of space. There is no sound in a vacuum of space," the guy says.

Steve goes back downstairs. In a little while, just as Steve is thinking about quietly jerking off again, the guy upstairs starts in. He clearly isn't trying to hold it down any. Steve can hear him talking to the monitor. Steve blushes, picturing the Red-haired Girl hearing him saying very similar things.

Instead Steve sends out emails to old clients, offering them Proven Customer Discounts. *You Know Who To Call, When You Need a Haul: Brotherman's*, he writes at the end of each. Most of them come back asking to please have their addresses purged from this list. Many simply write, *remove*. The guy upstairs orgasms. He goes off like a bear. There is brief silence, then Bob Barker's muffled voice fills the room.

Steve eats a Pepcid and goes outside to walk around the apartment complex with his hands behind his head to try and get rid of the cramp coming on in his gut. The bad thing about the Red-haired Girl is that she has a dog, an ugly little English bulldog named Lusya. She walks it constantly with all the other women in the complex who have dogs. She's told them about Steve. He imagines her telling them about him going at it up there, three to four solid hours. Every woman with a dog in the complex avoids him. When he walks past them in the halls they look at the floor and allow their menacing dogs to the farthest reaches of their leashes, close enough to feel their hot breath on his marinated fingers.

The Red-haired Girl, however, being complicated, does talk to him. She has this nice thing. She wanted to let him know that she could hear what he was doing by telling him she could hear him doing something else, in order to get him to stop doing what he was doing so loudly, but in a way so he thought she really didn't hear what he was doing, because that kind of embarrassed her. And when she sees him with the patch over his eye, she feigns concern. He doesn't know her name and she doesn't know his.

He keeps his hands behind his head—women notice hands—and tells her that he scratched the cornea at work. It's funny, he thinks, the loss of an eye doesn't really even bother him; the addition of a penny does. When they talk, while it is obvious she is trying to be nice, she maintains a nervous glance in her eye. Steve wonders if she has this with everyone. Lusya donates a half-hearted jump at his leg. Even her dog pretends to like him.

Evolutionarily speaking, Steve considers himself a fluke. He is short, not tall. Like his fingernails, his toenails are bad, though he has never bitten them. He is not particularly smart; is weird looking; and no good at sports or fighting. He compulsively has bad idea after bad idea, such as starting this hauling company now dying a brisk death. There's not much propulsion behind his orgasm.

"You were right you know," he says. "These apartments really do suck. I mean. I don't know if I should tell you this. But the guy upstairs from me…" Steve motions for her to come nearer. "I don't know if I should tell you this."

"Yeah," she says, and steps backward.

"He masturbates all day," Steve says, resisting the urge to make the universal hand signal for jerking off. "For hours and hours. It's so loud."

"Are you kidding me?" she says.

"No. It's terrible, like he's in the same room with me, which you have to admit if you've ever seen him, it's a scary thought. But I don't want to go up there and tell him I can hear that, you know."

"Yeah, it's awkward, or something."

"You're telling me. I wouldn't be a bit surprised if you could hear him straight through to your apartment."

"Hours and hours and hours?" she says.

"At least. And talking to the screen. *Oh baby, oh yeah baby.* It's enough to, I tell you. Freaking pathetic. I've heard him—and you know he's the only one up there—going *Rock with me. Rock with me. Suckle, suckle...*"

"I have in fact. Well, talk about embarrassing. I thought that was you." Her skin turns the exact shade of her hair and freckles, causing her freckles to temporarily disappear.

"Oh, no. No! You should—you can come up some time and listen. I mean just to prove it."

She immediately gets all apologetic. Her skin color deepens and deepens until it begins to brown. The shade of her skin overtakes the freckles and they resurface. She checks him out, seems to see him in a new light. She leans in, as if they're chuckling a secret. The dog rubs its butt against his boot.

"Do you smell hot sauce?" she asks.

There is an immediate, marked transformation in the way women with dogs around the complex relate to Steve. When he leaves that afternoon to pick up Jeremy, a blonde with a Newfoundland the size of a Yugo, a dog which she'd just yesterday allowed to plant both its front paws on his chest as he backed into a corner, waves hello at him, and when the Yugo goes for his hands, she jerks it back. "He's nothing," she says, "an absolute vagina monologue."

So Steve is as upbeat as a guy with a foreign body in him can be until they cruise around town checking their flyers. They discover all of them—at the gas stations, the COTA stops, the dump, the post office, fish camp, the industrial parks, in the Port-O-Lets at construction sites, Skyline Chili, Payless Shoes, the comic book store—covered up with Two Men And A Truck flyers. They append their flyers with super sticky double-sided tape, which ruins the Brotherman's flyers underneath.

"The miracle is we still have enough pennies to Xerox our own flyers," Jeremy says when they check the Community Bulletin Board at the PriceChopper, "with you going around eating them all." Jeremy scribbles on the Two Men flyers. On one he draws a little caricature of two stick-figure men buttfucking in parentheses. On others he writes: *I take umbrage AT your two frigging faces. I take umbrage AT your hauling. I take umbrage TO the Two Fags And A Buckity-Buck.*

"You're not getting what I'm saying," Steve says. "It worked. I should have blown that breath reader off the charts. All the tequila I put back. It could have been fifty percent I'm telling you."

"With your drunk driving ability then, it had to have been the signs. Just take off the signs." Jeremy knows what a terrible drunk driver Steve is, but, knowing what pride Steve takes in his supposed prowess, he keeps it quiet and never goes out for the serious drinking with him after work. The truth is Jeremy has been talking to some guys at the dump who haul things around the landfill about bringing him on. There is no shortage of things people don't want at the dump like there seems to be in the rest of the world.

"I'm not talking about why I got pulled over. That seems pretty obvious. I'm saying the penny fucked up the test."

Jeremy staples the new Brotherman's flyers over the defaced Two Men flyers.

"I don't know anything about a breathalyzer, brotherman. Or for that matter what a penny will do about it. What I know is if you'd blown one one-thousandth more, there'd be no business right about now. Then what would we do?" Jeremy would step up the pressure on the guys at the dump is what. Jeremy can't drive, but can the bitch haul. The guy is built like a small forklift. When not carrying anything he moves about as if he's falling backwards. He slants at forty-five degrees from knees to waist so that his feet always arrive somewhere before the rest of him. He's five foot four with arms that bear hug a Barcalounger. When he picks something up he sinks into himself; it's the only time his feet and head are in line. Steve interprets these qualities to mean that Jeremy can fight. Jeremy can haul. Jeremy likely intimidates. Jeremy cannot fight.

"If one single person on one single night sees these signs, and we get a job out of it, that's one job more we'd have than now. I'm not taking off the signs. I'd just like to pass this penny."

"It will pass," Jeremy says. "Have faith in that much."

Steve doesn't know.

Once they replace their fliers they do what they usually do: They buy a six-pack of Hollandia tall boys and go drink them at the park with their feet propped on the rear-view mirrors. The end of Brotherman's may be near anyway. Jeremy hands Steve his hot sauce from the glove compartment, and he unloads into his beer. He drinks the beer in hopes it will make him feel normal.

They wait for the mobile to ring. Jeremy searches phrase books and novels and newspapers from the library for passages quoting *umbrage at* something. Periodically he steps out and does pull-ups on the jungle gym. Steve worries about the penny and tries not to chew his nails. He rubs under his rib cage to see if he can feel anything and stains his T-shirt orange.

"You're worth more now," Jeremy says. "Think of it like that. Steve plus one cent." Then Jeremy says, "Tomorrow, let's go in early and ambush the Two Men at PriceChopper." Steve understands this to mean they will be kicking some Two Men ass in retribution for having one of their cop buddies pull him over, but

Jeremy intends only to clarify a grammatical point.

"What time?" Steve says.

"Early, make sure we don't miss them," he says.

"Sixish then?"

"Sixish."

Steve purchases sample packs of Metamucil and Ex-Lax and a single packet of apple and cinnamon oatmeal from the Dollar Store on the way home. That night he panics the panic of a man who may have something seriously wrong with him medically but does not have insurance. His jowls quiver. He's sweaty and pale in the bathroom mirror, white as the gauze eye patch. He washes his hands and he wants to bite them so bad they tremble. He rushes into the kitchen and soaks them again in the two bowls of hot sauce, beating his head on the table to the *Jeopardy* tune. He mixes fiber, oatmeal, and laxative in a bowl of boiling water. He breathes the steam, and when it's cool enough he eats.

Afterward he powers on the computer and takes out his polyethylene glove, coats it in cocoa butter, goes to one of the free movie sites and cranks up. He talks to the screen, imitating the voice of the guy upstairs, and when it's over he collapses into the lawn chair he uses as an office chair, then spends an hour on the toilet pushing, concentrating, pushing, before admitting failure, swallowing half a Xanax and falling deeply to sleep.

Based on what Steve told her, while this may seem farfetched, the Red-haired Girl hears Steve as she prepares for bed and watches the Weather Channel, slightly concerned by the TV's constant beeping because of severe incoming weather. She believes that it is the guy two floors up jerking off while talking to the screen, even though the sound seems to be coming from directly over her head. The walls and ceilings are thin enough, she believes, which is why the severe incoming weather concerns her.

Steve wakes to weather sirens and the taste of fingers. In his sleep, the fingers of his left hand—his favorite to chew for angle and bent—have migrated to his mouth. Outside it sounds like a bombing raid. He opens his window and the wind and rain whip through the room. The sirens are interspersed with a garbled message. He sticks his head out into the dark to hear better. Weather-warning megaphone speakers in the distance blare something that sounds like: *Lorena Bobbitt in area. Seek lover.*

He can barely hear knocking at the door. It's the Red-haired Girl, standing there holding a vanilla-scented candle.

"This is your wake-up call," she says. "The severe incoming weather is income. The whole building's in the basement."

Steve disappears to find his shoes. He slips his bare feet into his work boots. When he comes back she is standing in his living room. In the lightning flashes, he sees the hot sauce bowls on the kitchen table, the open tub of cocoa butter and the glove on the computer desk.

"We have the exact same space," she says. "And there is where the magic happens." She points to the ceiling.

He makes to get her out of the room fast, taking her by the waist. She interprets this as a forward move. She likes forward. They take the steps carefully in the dark, stopping only to let the guy upstairs brush by with a flashlight, his feet smacking the stairs like soft tomatoes.

The Red-haired girl enters the basement first. Her candle illuminates their neighbors and a goldmine of junk. Steve simply marvels for a moment. The remnants of who knows how many years of tenants' leftovers, rotten and mildewed from the moisture, well beyond any desirable condition. The mess is arranged in aisles. Their neighbors are situated among the aisles in little cliques. The women with dogs smile nervously and wave. Every person secretly chastises himself for saving the however-much per month to live in the flimsy-walled apartment building they all live in. An AM radio reports multiple tornadoes spotted in the area.

Steve takes the candle and the lead now. He wanders through lanes of wooden crates, old doors, paintings, battered suitcases, porch swings, mattresses, and box springs. There's ancient dressers and stacks of mismatched drawers, a foreign-looking shrunk, and couch beds—big, heavy, steel couch beds.

The Red-haired Girl takes Steve's arm. Her nails dig into his bicep. He registers their crispy quality. He looks down and is excited to find that he can see them reflecting the candle, finely shaped, perfectly manicured, the kind with a whitewall across the top and a lavender body. The Xanax emphasizes everything.

The Red-haired Girl stops him in front of a basement window. She points to a blanket underneath two sawhorses, where her bulldog Lusya is sitting. "Kind of a cool spot right?" she says.

"A room with a view," Steve says. Through the window they see the little shrubs lining the apartment building sideways in the wind.

The siren and the unintelligible announcement broken-records.

"What the hell are they trying to tell us?" Steve asks.

"The sky is plummeting," she says.

"I don't know your name," Steve says.

"You see me all the time," she says. "You must have some way of thinking of me."

"The Red-haired Girl," Steve says.

"You're the Creepy Cute Guy," she says. "Let's stick with those for now." Then she says, "Look." The little sideways shrubs are gone.

When he wakes up, he is horrified to discover his hand clawing up the Red-haired Girl's stockinged leg, catching and running as it goes. A purple light seeps in through the window, and the basement is quiet.

She interprets his gesture in a particular way and pulls herself out of the shredded stockings.

"Touch me," she says. Steve retracts his hands out of habit.

"I don't do that," Steve says. She interprets this in a particular way also. Steve is really shy and awkward about these things. She interprets him as forceful and direct.

She says something else then, which Steve cannot decipher: "Moose me," maybe.

Steve does what he believes is expected of him. He is intrigued to discover she tastes like lemon. Leaned against the foreign shrunk in the back corner the guy upstairs begins masturbating, for the first time in his life, quietly, without even a whisper as he watches them through the sawhorses.

Soon Steve desires different textures. He bites, which seems to be the thing. Her body flops around. He keeps on biting, all the way down her leg, her ankle for a while, back up, knee, hip bone, nipple one, nipple two, lip, ear, lymph node, neck fold. She goes for it. When he moves down her arm—shoulder, elbow, wrist—something tells him just to get what it is he's after. He starts small, the hard, tender nail on the end of her pinky. He nips that off in two clean bites, no tearing, practiced. Then goes the thumb. He decimates her lovely nails, during which she orgasms thrice.

The Red-haired Girl, while genuinely liking this, does not expect that it will constitute the main activity of a sexual relationship with Steve. The guy upstairs ejaculates all over himself, without making a sound.

Steve would say that he notices the penny less today. But no one is asking. Jeremy is writing on a piece of paper as Steve maneuvers the F-150 through the twilight, around fallen power lines and trees, to the PriceChopper. He parks at the other end of the parking lot, away from the automatic doors, where they have a clear view of the Community Bulletin Board.

Six thirty rolls around and then seven. Steve gets on the mobile and calls the landlord. He explains to him that he just happened to seek shelter in the basement last night and couldn't help noticing all the junk. He also just happens to run a hauling company if he's interested in getting rid of it. The landlord seems receptive, asks for the name of his business. There is a negotiating period. Steve wants two months rent. The landlord says he'll meet him there to discuss it further this week, but right now, he could actually use Brotherman's to haul away the detritus tornados dropped onto a number of his properties. Steve says he thinks they could find time in their schedules to do that today.

"We got work," he says, turning to Jeremy. Jeremy is too nervous to answer.

A truck parks in the fire lane.

Steve and Jeremy look at each other. They get out. The Two Men—caught taping over their flyers—notice them from across the parking lot. They recognize the duo from having themselves once staked out the competition for the same purpose they are now being staked out. When they'd seen Jeremy, they'd called that plan off. Now they come toward them, full stride.

And this is when Jeremy stops. Steve stops too, figuring that Jeremy is bearing the brunt of this thing.

Jeremy holds up the piece of paper he's been working on and clears his throat. The Two Men eye them from across the parking lot like in an old Western. Jeremy begins to read:

"Mr. Jack Maldon shook hands with me; but not very warmly, I believed; and with an air of languid patronage, at which I secretly took great umbrage…A wife…who properly conducted her economy, should take no umbrage at such little fancies of her husband, but be always certain that he would return…"

Steve ignores what he thinks he mistakenly perceives as a tremble in Jeremy's voice. He is not mistaken.

"How fathers should not draw too ready rein/Nor sons take umbrage in a trice/At father's counsels…"

Steve recognizes fully the miscalculation made here when the Two Men recommence their approach and the sound of footsteps in hasty retreat appears first from beside him, where Jeremy was just a moment ago standing, reciting his speech, then from further and further behind him. On his stocky legs, Jeremy trucks through the parking lot. Whereas normally he is slanted backward, he is now full-frontal. He moves well through the morning. Steve wonders where exactly he plans to go. Jeremy figures he was on his way out anyhow.

The Two Men stand in front of Steve looking for an answer.

"There's so many things you can do with a truck," he offers.

Just one of the Two Men, the one who *looks* like he used to be a cop, takes his shot, which Steve manages to block, but then the other hand of the one Two Men comes as if out of nowhere because the eye patch makes this huge blind spot. Steve stays where he falls on the wet asphalt. His teeth feel pushed. His mouth, drowned in blood, tastes of penny.

The Two Men look down on him as the grocery store cop waltzes over.

"This poor guy's keeling here," says one of the Two Men.

"Must of just fell," one of them said.

"Must of," says the other.

They both high-five the cop.

…he dreams about the Red-haired Girl's fingernails. In the dream he vividly experiences the crack as they snap between his teeth…to gauge he puts his own thumb in his mouth and pushes around on his teeth. They are all there, but the front ones give, roughly as much play as the steering wheel on the F-150…the cop returns with a fat man dressed in grocery store manager clothes. They look down at him. "Might be he's a vagrant," the cop says. "Hey," the manager says. "You speak English? No loitering."

For a little while Steve has a scratched cornea, a penny impacted in his esophagus, and a mild concussion all at the same time. Not to mention loose teeth. A nurse has coated his fingernails in iodine interpreting them as injuries based on their assumption that he's homeless. Then he's in the radiology suite and the doctor is cramming a balloon down his throat (fluoroscopic balloon catheter extraction), then inflating the balloon (which is like taking a deep breath without taking the breath), and pushing the penny into his stomach.

They put him in a bed next to a kid who has swallowed a small light bulb. They apparently group like injuries together in emergency rooms. They want to keep him there for a couple hours, and since no one has brought up the whole insurance thing yet he doesn't talk too much. If they figure he's a charity case let them figure he's a charity case. The kid keeps hogging the bathroom in their area to vomit. And after one trip he emerges smiling and holding a little unbroken bulb between his thumb and index finger.

When Steve takes his turn, he has what he would consider to be your standard, normal bowel movement. There is no plink, nor any feeling like you might expect with a penny coming out of your ass. He does not even think he's expelled it, but he checks anyway, and there it is submerged in the bottom of the pot. It seems larger and shinier than he'd expected. Steve has never seen a penny so bright and shiny.

He uses the back end of the toilet scrubber to slide it up the porcelain. Once he gets it near the rim he reaches in and peels it off. He washes the penny and his hands under the cool water from the hospital sink. He dries off with the thick brown paper towels and holds the penny up to the fluorescent light.

In that light Steve catches sight of his fingernails. Underneath the hot sauce and iodine they are beginning to grow over, maybe for the first time, with small but definite frosty white tips, still jagged but smoothing. The trajectory is clear. They will grow up and through the inflamed pink cuticle. They will have to. There is nowhere else to go. This will be painful, but the final result is something that Steve wants to admire. He wants to see that. For the time being at least, he thinks, I am holding in my hands eleven accomplishments.

❧ *This is Not About Me* ☙

BILL PETTITT

I was born with an extra finger on my right hand. Some kind of defect or something. It was never a big deal. I might have been shier than the average kid, but kids tend to be shy. The finger was small, just a little growth below the pinky. It didn't have a joint of its own, not even at the base where it was attached to my hand, and this rendered it fairly useless as fingers go.

My mother, who smoked weed in college, always insisted that the finger was a sign of evolutionary progress. She said I was the living hope that our human race is unfinished, that we may eventually civilize ourselves and learn to live together in peace and harmony. That's an awful lot of faith to place on an appendage the size of a grape, but that's my mother. This is the woman who still receives financial advice from her grandfather, a retired appliance salesman who has been dead for nearly twenty years. But then I'm not saying she's wrong either. I'm a fairly mild mannered guy and I've never killed anyone, so who's to say I *haven't* evolved in some small but significant way? I mean really. I watch the news. I know what people can do to each other.

My wife never liked the finger. It creeped her out. She succeeded, for the most part, in ignoring its existence and she was very instructional in helping me keep the thing away from her. But every once in a while, during the act of love for example, I'd touch her the wrong way and then she'd simply flip. I also had a bad habit of tapping the finger against the table while we were eating. This drove her up the wall. She'd toss her knife and fork onto her plate and say, "Stewart, if you're trying to keep me thin, then by all means keep on tapping because I think I'm going to puke." But for the most part we got along. And even if the finger wasn't exactly the Second Coming, as my mother liked to think, it was one heck of a lot better than, say, an extra nose or an extra arm or even—could you imagine?—an extra heart. Everyone has fingers, quite a few of them, and up until this night I want to talk about, the night my wife cut it off with a buzz saw, I simply had one more finger than most everyone else.

My wife and I were married nine years ago. I married her because I loved her, in spite of the fine dark hairs which grew above her upper lip. I never mentioned them to her, these hairs, but I'm sure I must have done something to make her feel ugly or unwanted because they disappeared shortly after the honeymoon. She always was intuitive that way.

We never had children. Never tried. Instead we had our house. It consumed nearly all of our energy. It was a turn-of-the-century bungalow in Boise's North End. The thing was a piece of shit when we bought it. The roof was caving in, the basement damp and moldy, and the plumbing creaked and groaned as if the whole house might explode. But the house had potential and I think that's why we fell in love with it. It was a project. My wife had a brilliant eye for design and she was also handy with the power tools. We expanded the kitchen, added a master bath with a classic claw foot tub, pulled up the floor, knocked down walls, and as a result we lived in a perpetual mess of saw dust and plaster rubble. But the strange thing was we didn't see the mess. We saw the house in its perfect state, as it would someday be, once the projects were all finished. In a strange way it was like living in a mansion. Or even better, it was like living in a dream, which is precisely what it was.

But then one day we looked around and the house was done. It had, in fact, been done for quite some time. And once the projects ceased things started to change between us. We became more aware of each other, and not in my mother's Zen-hippie-higher-planes-of-awareness type of way. Just plain physical awareness. We were constantly bumping into each other in the hallways, squeezing through doorways at the same time, needing the toilet right after the other sat down. Even the tub became too small for the both of us. We needed another project, but I doubt we recognized this at the time. What we did recognize was a general dissatisfaction—with ourselves or with each other we couldn't really say.

One night we were over at Edwardo's hot tub party for a game of co-ed naked Scrabble. This was something we used to do with our friends about once every month or so and it's exactly as it sounds. We had a floating plastic Scrabble board and Edwardo, our oldest friend and the one who introduced us to each other in the first place, owns a hot tub in his back yard. There were usually six to eight of us, all of us married except for Edwardo, who always seemed to have a different girl. We rarely finished a game because the water was too hot. But that was hardly the point. We were young, and we fancied ourselves to be rather progressive in a not so progressive town, and besides it was awfully fun. But perhaps in the end it wasn't such a splendid idea.

The game began with Edwardo's inevitable joke that I should start with one more tile than everyone else.

"An extra tile for an extra digit," he said, "it's only fair."

My wife hated these jokes and Edwardo knew that. But when she refused to smile, or even groan disapprovingly, he slid up next to her and whispered, loud enough for all of us to hear, "too bad it wasn't an extra something *else*, eh?" This, too, was a tired joke. They all were. There were jokes about high sixes, jokes about gloves—these were always popular—there were jokes about the piggies going to market and staying home but what did *this* one do? I'd heard them all my life and they never changed no matter where I went. And I'm sure, once Edwardo got going that night, we heard them all again, until finally my wife claimed that she was done, that she was too hot to play anymore, and she stood up to climb out of the tub.

Now my wife, it must be said, has an extremely thick bush of hair between her legs which comes all the way up to her navel and clear out to her hip bones. I'd always found it sexy in the past, but these hairs can hold ridiculous amounts of water and it seemed to take forever for her bush to drain. This, as you might imagine, interrupted our game. We sat there politely, arranging and rearranging our Scrabble tiles, pretending not to notice the gurgling kerplunck, kerplunck, kerpluck of water falling back into the tub. And I remember thinking—I actually thought this at the time—that if I'd brought Teaonna from work to this hot tub party, if I'd brought Teaonna and *not* my wife, then I'd be spared these embarrassing kerpluncks right now because Teaonna from work, as everybody in the office knew, wore a neatly trimmed heart-shaped bush and waxed her under region.

I'd tried, several times, to get my wife to wax like that but she always balked and said, you're crazy Stewart. She said, you don't really want me to be like those silly, giggly girls who show up with Edwardo at his parties. And, of course, that's precisely what I wanted her to be like, though these *girls*, as she called them, were mostly twenty-something paralegals, some of them married, and they really didn't seem all that silly to me. And the truth was, I didn't *want* to think about these girls. Not like that. All I'd ever wanted was to be one of those perfect, devoted husbands who never ever, *ever* thought about another woman. And it seemed to me that my wife should want that too, which is why I asked her to do that waxing thing. So I could keep coming to these parties, look at these girls and think to myself, sure they're sexy and all, but what have they got on my wife? On my darling, loving wife? I tried to explain this to her but she responded with something that TV psychologist was always saying to get cheers from his audience—that if I really loved her I should love her *just the way she is.* Which really, in my opinion, missed the whole goddamn point.

For Christmas I bought her one of those new high tech tread master walking machines and she wasn't offended at all. Not at first. She was actually excited about the prospect of getting herself into shape and for the first few months she worked out half an hour every day. But then she became busy with work and she missed a day, and then another, and soon the machine seemed more like a burden to her than an opportunity. She probably would have sold it or put it in the basement, but because it had been a gift from me, the thing stayed in the living room and tormented her. She grew resentful of it, and then turned that resentment on me. Until she finally let me have it at dinner one night. Just as she was about to take a bite of her lasagna, she said, "Don't look at me that way," and when I asked "what way?" she said, "you know," and then she told me I was weighing her with my eyes, which wasn't true at all because if anything I'd always thought she could gain a few pounds, but saying this only sounded like that thing you're supposed to say when your wife is accusing you of thinking she's fat. And then she said I'd been doing it since Christmas, ever since I bought her that horrendous machine. And when I told her, fine, we'd just get rid of the machine, she looked at me suspiciously as if she didn't quite believe me and suddenly, out of nowhere, she said, "You're having an affair with that little chickadee from work, aren't you?"

Now Teaonna from work, the one who did that waxing thing, did not have a problem with my extra finger. She called it the *dinky pinky*, which was a little too cutesy for my taste. But I put up with it because I'd discovered recently that I could wiggle the finger just enough to make her squeal when I tickled her ribs. This was the first practical use I'd found for the thing since grade school when I harnessed a great amount of attention chasing the girls screaming and crying around the playground. Technically, I suppose, Teaonna from work could have had me fired for sexual harassment. But she, herself, claimed I'd found a loophole in the sex laws. "You can't harass someone," she told me, "with an appendage that isn't in the books." She was sitting on the edge of my desk when she said this. Her strong, girlish legs were crossed, her short skirt was hiked just a little too far up her thigh. This was as far as we'd gotten. I hadn't slept with her and already I knew I wouldn't. For one thing, I was deathly afraid she'd change her mind at the last minute and then she really could get me fired. The other reason, I suppose, was that I still loved my wife. But the fascination was there and it's true I was guilty of comparing my wife to another woman.

So then one night—and this is the night I want to talk about—my wife spent an hour and a half on the phone with her best friend, Alicia the librarian. When she was done she came into the living room, plopped herself on the easy chair and crossed her arms. This was her way of telling me I was in some kind of trouble.

"Guess what Donny did today?" she said.

"Don't know," I said. And then, because I also didn't know who Donny was, I said, "who's Donny?"

This was not the right thing to say, because as it turns out, Donny is Alicia the librarian's husband and I was supposed to know this already because he'd been to our house at least five times in the past few years which means that somewhere scattered around my desk were at least five real estate cards boasting Donny's slick cheesy grin.

"Donny made a cabinet for the kitchen," my wife said, and when I said, "A cabinet," trying to sound interested, she said "Yes, a little one for the wall, and he made it from scratch too."

I could see where this was going and I wanted to put a stop to it before it got there, so I said, "I don't really know how to make cabinets," and this was true.

But my wife continued. "He kept it a secret until he was done," she said, "and it's not even her birthday or anything. Just a surprise. Just a nice surprise."

It was difficult, at this point, not to hate Donny the real estate agent, and his crafty hands, just a little. "I suppose I could learn," I offered, "if you really want a cabinet I could take a wood class or something."

That's when my wife lost it. "I don't want a fucking cabinet," she said, "will you shut up about the cabinet, already?" As soon as she said it, her jaw snapped shut. She was as startled as I was. We sat and looked at each other, both of us a little bewildered. My wife shifted herself in the easy chair as if the simple act of sitting were causing her physical pain.

"All right," I said, "tell me what's wrong. Something's a matter obviously."

"I don't know. It's just stupid."

"What's stupid?"

"Nothing," she said, "Just drop it."

I nodded, ok, and then I dropped it.

"It's just that you never do anything like that," she said, "you never made things for me without telling me."

I said, "That's kind of a specific thing, isn't it?"

She shifted in the chair again, and when she did so she winced, sucked in a breath of air, and said, "Now what's that supposed to mean?"

And what I meant was that Donny the real estate agent had gone and done this very specific thing and now it was something I never did. I was suddenly that type of husband who never makes cabinets for his wife. And when I explained this to her she said, "This isn't about Donny, this is about you and never surprising me with anything," and I said "It *does* seem to be a *little* about Donny," at which point she blew up again and said "will you shut up about Donny already?"

I noticed one of her hands was resting over her crotch and when she saw me looking she quickly moved her hand to her thigh.

"I just wish that for once I could be the one making that phone call telling all my girlfriends about something nice you did for me," she said, "a wife should be able to do that once in a while."

I accused her, then, of wanting me to be someone I'm not, and to make it worse that *someone* had to be Donny, of all people, Alecia the librarian's redneck husband.

Her lower eyelids pooled up, which was odd because she is not the break-down-into-tears type of woman. Her fingers moved from her thigh back to her crotch, though I suspect she was unaware of this. I did feel bad. Not that I didn't feel I was right, but I think sometimes if you really love someone, and I did love my wife, then being right has little to do with anything.

So I stood and walked over to her and placed my left hand, my normal hand, on her shoulder.

"I didn't mean it," I said.

But she pulled her shoulder away and said, "Fuck you and your sympathy, Stewart, you don't even know what this is about." Her fingers were still down there clutching tightly to her crotch, white knuckles and all. She said, "the thing I hate, is that you think I'm crying because of what you just said, but that's not it at all. It's this *fucking* rash, Stewart. This *fucking* rash that doesn't seem like it will ever go away."

And what could I say to her then? She'd gone and done it, just like I'd been hoping. An elaborate surprise for me on an ordinary day. This is what she'd been trying to tell me. Just a nice surprise. And yet everything had gone wrong for her. She was in terrible pain down there, I could see that, and there was nothing she could do about it. She couldn't postpone the surprise, or pretend she'd never done it, and on top of that I had come home and made a mess of everything. I pushed her past the breaking point on a day when she lacked the ammunition to strike back. For how do you really stand up to your husband when you've just shaved a mountain of pubic hair from your own body just to satisfy his stupid fantasies? Looking back, of course, I can see she'd been trying to save us, to rekindle something we'd lost long before. But at the moment I still couldn't see how far we'd come, and so I didn't know how much we'd already lost.

Perhaps if I'd known, I'd have tried harder. Instead I tried to resolve the problem sensibly.

"I'll get you some cortisone cream," I said, grabbing my jacket and kissing her on the top of the head, "I'll try to get the strongest stuff they have." And she didn't say a word as I walked out the door.

That night in bed we were both awfully cautious with each other. I was, perhaps, acting too tender and doting, asking if it still hurt, was she ok? Was there anything I could do for her? I even told her it was a really sweet thing she'd done and that I appreciated it.

This didn't go over so well. "Sweet?" she said, "Stewart, aren't you even going to pretend that what I've done is sexy to you?"

"Of course it's sexy," I said, caressing her cheek with the back of my hand.

"It's clear," she replied, "that you can barely contain yourself."

"But you're in pain," I said, "I just assumed you wouldn't want to, tonight."

She turned her back to me. "Well you assumed correctly," she said, "but you could at least have given me the pleasure of turning you down."

In the nine years we'd been husband and wife, this was the first time we went to bed without resolving the issue or coming to some sort of understanding. This was perhaps a mistake on our part, though I doubt this, alone, was responsible for everything which transpired. Later, my wife would describe it as some sort of dream, even though she was aware of what she was doing. She said at some point in the night I rolled over and my right hand fell over her face and that she woke up with my extra finger in her mouth, and how it seemed to be suffocating her, choking her, killing her, and how suddenly that finger seemed to be at the root of all her problems and all she could think about, then, was getting the thing as far away from her as possible.

When I think back on it now, I don't remember the pain. I remember the sound of the saw and I remember opening my eyes to see that look on my wife's face. It was something like terror, confusion and excitement all mixed together. The buzz saw cut out before I knew what had happened, as if the blade simply choked.

What followed was a strange, charged silence. I was lying on my back and my wife was on top of me, straddling me, and in her hand was that saw.

"What?" I said.

My wife's reply was just as vague.

"Yep," she said.

Her face twisted into that strange, bloated expression you make when you're trying not to laugh. And then I, too, was trying not to laugh. I doubt we really found anything amusing about this, but this thing had just happened, this very *very* big thing, and it was still so new that we were not yet forced to deal with the consequences of it. So I simply said it again.

"*What?*"

And she said it again, "*Yep!*"

And by then, my wound was gushing like you wouldn't believe. Speckles of red were splattered all over her face. Her night gown was so wet with blood that her nipples showed through. And suddenly the sheer horror of the situation caught up with me. I grabbed my wife by the waist and threw her off of me. She fell from the bed with a painful thud, and then I was living through a chaotic blur. My wife was bawling and I was screaming all sorts of obscenities, some directed towards her, but most directed towards my wound and the missing finger, which, as it turned out, was really missing. I mean it was gone. Nowhere to be found. I tore the bloody sheets off the bed, I threw the mattress so that it flipped over and landed on my wife, I knocked over the bed stand, and the whole time I was screaming, "where is my finger? What the hell did you do with my finger?" In my mania that lost finger became the most important thing in the world.

Blood was everywhere and my wife had wiggled her way out from under the mattress and for some reason she was searching for the finger as well, searching frantically, throwing the sheets, unloading the drawers and generally adding to the confusion. "I don't know," she kept telling me, "I don't know. I don't know. *I don't know.*" And it was unclear whether this referred to the whereabouts of my missing finger or whether she meant she didn't know why she had just done this terrible thing.

But it was my wife who eventually discovered the finger. It was wedged deep inside the buzz saw. It was wedged so tight we couldn't get it out. This, perhaps, proved to be a good thing, almost a calming thing. We sat on the corner of the box spring and turned it into a project, the two of us. We tried screw drivers and coat hangers. We tried to suck it out with the Shop Vac. We even tried turning the saw back on but the blade was firmly jammed. I would have sat there digging for the finger all night long if my wife hadn't taken action. She took the buzz saw and disappeared into the kitchen and I could hear the sharp crunch of ice cubes falling over the saw.

I grabbed a corner of the bed sheet and wrapped it around my hand. I wrapped it several times and let the remainder of the sheet trail behind me. When I joined my wife in the kitchen she was filling our large blue Igloo cooler with ice. The saw was inside, half buried.

"Quick," she snapped, "we're losing time." She was on a mission now. You could see it in her body. From then on, my wife was in charge, driving through stop signs and weaving around cars. When we arrived at the emergency room she rushed forward and heaved the cooler onto the counter.

"My husband's finger is in there," she said, "we need to have it sewn back on."

Soon there were doctors and nurses everywhere and I lost

track of my wife in the shuffle. I was placed on a gurney and
rolled through several halls lying on my back. In the operating
room, the nurses shot me up with all sorts of drugs which made
the ceiling lights throb. One of the nurses retrieved a pair of
scissors and cut the bloody sheet from my hand. The hospital
staff, there must have been six or seven of them, converged on
my hand with sponges and needles and gauze.

Down by my feet I could hear my wife and several other voices, and when I looked up, I could see that they were working on
the saw, trying to fish my finger out with a stainless steel hook,
and for some reason I found myself wincing every time they
shoved that hook down inside the saw.

Then several things happened. The nurses realized, almost
collectively, that I still possessed five full fingers. The commo-
tion stopped at once, the room grew quiet with confusion and
just then the doctor working on the saw retrieved the finger. He
dropped it into a stainless steel tray. This created a tiny metallic
clink which, as I remember it, was the only sound in the room.
The silence lasted another moment, everyone glancing around
the room, at each other, then down at me. Then everyone started
talking at once. How did you wound your hand? Whose finger is
in that tray? Can you still move your fingers? Are you allergic to
penicillin? And for the love of God, *whose finger is in that tray?*

My wife took the finger, walked over to my side and grabbed
my right hand. "My husband has six fingers," she said, touching
them one at a time starting with the thumb, "One, two, three,
four, five, and six," she said, holding up the severed finger. "Now
get to work and sew this thing back on." She pressed the finger
against my wound as if it were that easy, as if we can be dis-
mantled and put back together with the ease of a model airplane
or an old rickety house. She continued to apply pressure until I
yelped out in pain and tried to withdraw my hand. But she was

holding me so tightly that I only succeeded in pulling her closer to me. All of her strength and energy was focused in on my hand. I could see something like desperation in her eyes.

"Will someone come over here and help me?" she said, "will you fucking doctors just do your fucking job?" She said this while keeping her eyes fixed on my hand. By now the pain was nearly unbearable and I could feel myself growing faint. But no one came to help her out. The nurses were standing around waiting for the doctors and the doctors were having a quiet discussion in the corner. So I reached over with my other hand and I placed it lightly on my wife's hands. They were shaking from the sheer exertion of trying to put me back together.

"It's ok," I said, "you did the best you could do."

But my wife shook her head, stubbornly, and pressed even harder. A shock of pain charged up my arm and the last thing I heard before I drifted away were my wife's pleading cries for help.

The doctors never did sew my finger back on, though they did an excellent job of reconstructing the side of my hand so it's difficult to tell that I ever had an extra finger. It all had something to do with insurance and whether or not the surgery was necessary or cosmetic. "If it had been your thumb," the doctor explained, apologetically, "or even your real pinky, we might have been able to accommodate you."

My mother, of course, was appalled. "Criminals," she exclaimed, "Thieving meddlesome criminals. That's the corporations. Sitting in their Manhattan high rises dictating who you should be and what you should look like and how many fingers a person should have."

She's right, of course. But I didn't have the heart to tell her she's been doing the same thing from the day I was born. I suppose we all do it. Changing and fixing and altering each other to complement some perfect image we have. It seems to me now that this is one of the most violent things we do to each other. We don't always bleed, but I wonder if things would be easier if we did. Perhaps, if we could actually see the wounds we leave behind us, then we really could learn to live in peace and harmony like my mother says.

As for me and my wife, I'd like to say that we learned our lesson, that we learned to follow the advice of those TV psychologists and simply accept each other for who we were. But the stark reality is that we fell in love for a reason. It was like that house we bought as newly weds. We never really loved that house, not even when it was done. It was the project we loved, the possibility of something better. And yet that possibility kept us happy for nine years. Maybe that's more than anyone can hope for.

I can't tell anymore if that's such a bad thing. I must say I'm enjoying the average normality of having ten fingers and I am sincerely grateful to my wife for that. And I think, in some strange way, all the blood and the pain and the trip to the emergency room paved the way for a very pleasant and amicable divorce. No fighting or yelling, only the appropriate amount of tears to let us know we were doing the right thing. We still see each other regularly, and now we share a different kind of love. It's a nostalgic love, free from promise or possibility, and therefore complete in its own way.

But I'm jumping too far ahead. Because the story doesn't end with an ex-husband and an ex-wife politely sipping coffee over neutral talk at a neutral cafe. This story ends, rather appropriately I think, in our bedroom, on our bed, shortly after we returned from the hospital. This was during the few remaining hours of that night. The streets outside were pitch black. My hand was freshly sewn and bandaged and the house was still torn apart and bloody from all that had taken place just a few hours before.

We stepped into the house. Quietly. Carefully. Politely. Because after all, how are a husband and wife supposed to return home at the end of a night like that one? My wife put down her keys and began to remove her coat, and I immediately stepped to her aide. I even said, "here, let me help you with that," and she even responded with, "thanks, that's very kind of you." And even though it was difficult with my hand bandaged up, I managed to remove her coat and hang it neatly in the closet. The hanger quietly went clink when it hit the solid metal bar. And then I turned around and we were standing there, not looking at each other and not talking, and there was really nothing left to say or do and soon, we knew, the sun would come up, and then it would be day, and that would be a day busy with washing and cleaning the house, which in turn would just be our own silent way of ending things in the very same fashion we started things years before.

But daylight was still a good fifteen minutes away, maybe a full-half hour, and we were standing in the foyer not talking to each other, and suddenly my wife looked up at me, as if startled by an idea, and she said, "Stewart, there's nothing we really can do but to make love right now," and she must have known I was going to protest, or say something reasonable or proper or polite, because she rushed over to me and kissed me on the lips, pressing her body against mine until I was backed all the way up against the closet wall and I was surrounded by coats and the rubber scent of rain jackets and the warmth of her lips, and then she paused for a moment, breathless, and she said "I'm still shaved down there, I'm just the way you wanted me," and it was kind of a sad thing to say but also a little bit playful and joking.

She smiled at me then, and it felt so damn good to see her smile, to see the gentle promise of her lips, but also the relief—the great overwhelming relief—of postponing for a little while what needed to come later. And so I kissed her back. And that's how we ended up on our bed, which was just a naked blood-stained mattress, but we were completely oblivious of that at the time. And we made love with such fury that the wound on my hand opened up again and seeped through the bandage and we didn't notice. We made love with such fury, that we didn't notice the roughness of my wife's stubble, tearing at our skin like sandpaper until we were bleeding down there too. And yet I believe in this moment, we were really truly in love. I believe this, even now looking back on it, without the cloud of passion to influence my heart. It was a different kind of love, to be sure. No longer the love of promise and possibility, and it was not yet that nostalgic love that would come to us later. But I do believe we arrived at the same place that night. We were in love because this was our house and we had fixed it up together and because that was a real thing. We were in love because we both found ourselves, for the moment, embodying the image of the other's desire and because we both felt the loss and the relief of having arrived there at last. And we were in love because the first pink rays of the rising sun were peeking through the window and because things could never be the same for us again.

Kleebe

PETER PAUL SMITH

"My whole life I've been running away from my balls," Kleebe told the bartender, stunning himself with the clarity of the insight. Here at last was the essential truth at the core of his existence; the fault was not in himself but in his testes. The bartender sleeved another glass onto the spinning brush in the sink full of suds. One local man, a regular, occupied his regular stool at the far end of the bar and two younger men, in their thirties, also spending the night down the road at the motel, played 50 cent-a-rack pool under the faux leaded glass Grain Belt Beer light.

My whole life, thought Kleebe; Jesus Christ, my whole fucking life. And now I figure it out; now that my balls are shriveled and useless. The wisdom of the ages falls into my lap and I can't even get wood.

"Come to terms with your balls, boys." That's what he'd have them chisel into his stone. "Don't let your balls lead you around by the nose."

"Gimme 'nother," Kleebe said.

The bartender, arms wet to the elbows, straightened up, wiped his hands on the front of his t-shirt and reached for the quart of

Wild Turkey on the back bar.

"Know what I wish?" Kleebe asked as the man poured, "I wish you could do like they do on Super Millionaire and help me phone a friend. I want to talk with Bobby Bindle. Want to tell him to stop running away from his balls."

Suds slid down the flag on the bartender's t-shirt.

"Live free or die," it said across the top of the flag.

Bindle would appreciate Kleebe's new-found wisdom. Bindle, witness to and partner in all that second class womanizing back then—when they were younger, if not exactly young. Most of those small town factory girls were grandmothers now, with grandsons named Dustin and Brandon riding dirtbikes and wearing sleeveless t-shirts with flags on the front. Live free or die.

Bindle. Bindle of the Viking Lounge at the Holiday Inn down the road in Wilmar. Bindle, with his eye out for that one special drunk woman with low self esteem who would take both of them home at closing time and introduce Kleebe to her sleep-addled room mate in the rumpled rayon nightie.

"We'll take it from here," his balls would tell him if the room-mate seemed willing to accommodate a drunk stranger. "We'll drive. Leave that lousy excuse for a boner in the front seat with us. Get in the back. Take a nap. We'll let you know when it's your turn to drive."

"You have low self esteem?" his balls might ask the sleepy roommate. "What a coincidence. We have low self esteem too."

And his balls would hang and glitter in the center of things like a cheap-assed disco ball over a road house dance floor while the sordid little coupling played itself out, becoming a montage of furtive gropes, squeezes, blurred bits and urges—a drunk-in-the-funhouse montage ending in a dull, turgorless orgasm and mutual disappointment.

"I'll have number three with whole wheat toast," he would tell the all night waitress at Perkins as he waited for Bindle to show up afterwards.

Most nights, Bindle never showed. Most nights Kleebe found his way back to the motel and fell across his bed and slept with one foot on the floor to keep the room from spinning.

The smaller of the two pool players swaggered around the far corner of the table, lined up the eight-ball and drilled it hard into the corner pocket—hard as if he were breaking a new rack.

"Take that, you bastard," the rooster of a man said. "Eat shit and die."

He let the cue slide back down through his right hand until the butt rested on the floor and he held his left hand out, palm up toward the other player.

"Pay up, sucker," he said cockily.

The other player, hulking, pulled a money clip from the pocket of his tailored pants, opened the roll of bills and peeled off a five.

"Luck," said the big man. "100% pure luck. Let's go again."

"One more," said the small man. "Just one more. Then we're going out to The Silo and getting laid."

"'Nother," Kleebe said to the bartender, Kleebe brooding a bit now at the unfairness of this sudden late middle age. Here he was, still on the road, covering the same territory, repping the same lines to the same customers; doing business with the customer's children now and, in one case, with the grandchildren of his original customers. Only the motels had changed, with his favorites, the little, flat-roofed, family owned places, mostly abandoned, burnt out, rotting, picture windows shattered, doors hanging by a single hinge. Prairie grass grew tall through the cracks in the parking lots.

The bartender poured Kleebe another.

When Kleebe was younger, he used to get drunker. He used to walk away from those small town motels on summer nights, down the road, out from under the last street light with its aura of gnats and swooping bats, into the dark of the prairie and he used to kneel on the concrete like a Muslim at prayer and put his ear to the pavement and listen. It was all connected; every mile of road, every street, every alley every driveway from coast to coast. He could hear all the parties and arguments, all the coupling and mayhem. The whole shooting match, including every woman who had ever tolerated him, all of it right there, connected to him through the concrete.

He didn't get drunk as much these days. The last time he had put his ear to anything it had been the cheap, thin paper on top of the examining table as Doc Timmons checked his prostate.

"A little on the plumpish side," Doc announced, withdrawing his finger, snapping the latex glove off and turning to the sink to wash his hands. "Let's keep an eye on it. Let's check it again in six months."

Not fair. Not fair at all. Everything was a little on the plumpish side now, including his nerfy memories of Nora, she who, even forty years later, truly had been the one. A little plumpish, his memories of the good times. Plumpish, too, his memory of how they said good-by. He left knowing it was over for good, but he hadn't really felt wronged until her letter arrived.

Now their past, a past he was certain meant nothing to Nora, was a newsreel; a cavalcade of plumpish little incidents, going grainy with age, the reasons for happiness or remorse becoming less distinct with each showing. Now he was a fifty-seven year old man on a barstool with a plumpish prostate and a plumpish heart tethered to a fading memory of a young woman in hippie era clothes, everything outmoded now, belonging to the past. He could hardly remember her face. The sound of her voice was gone for good.

And after Nora, the deluge. Never again anything real; never again anything heart to heart.

"I sense you have feelings of ambivalence for me," a college professor once told Kleebe in the cold gray light of a December dawn in Minneapolis. He was sitting on her hope chest, pulling his cheap black cotton socks on. Homely, pear shaped, freshly showered, wearing threadbare cotton panties that rose well past her hips and hid her navel, a frayed brassiere covering her meager breasts, backlit by the sixty-watt light falling into the room from her closet, she looked like a blow-up Socko The Clown toy.

"Maybe we shouldn't do this any more … Until you work some of this … stuff … out," she said. She opened her hands palms up and shrugged.

And they hadn't done that for a long time and when they resumed, he still hadn't worked anything out.

Ambivalence, Kleebe smirked into his glass. If ambivalence meant running after women and running away from his balls, he had had feelings of ambivalence for her.

"Do *you* want to marry me?" another woman asked him one New Years Eve. "I'll be 34 this year. My biological clock isn't ticking. It's gonging, for Christ's sake."

They were drunk and in bed and the New Year had begun with a mistimed, less than satisfying bit of sex. She forgave him his ineptitude, just like she forgave him his other faults—faults for which he could not forgive himself—and because she forgave him he did not want to marry her.

The next man married her. Kleebe read the announcement, a printed card that arrived in an envelope addressed in her hand, as he stood by the mailboxes in the foyer of his apartment building. It was raining outside—a cold, steady October rain that stripped the last leaves from the trees. When he had first seen the envelope, he had thought she had wanted to get back together.

He used to travel his territory with a case of Wild Turkey on the floor of the back seat at Christmas time. He used to drive with one hand on the wheel and the other flipping through legal pads full of notes about his customers.

He didn't need notes where Tess Howell was concerned, and that one year, dropping by with a bottle between Christmas and New Year's, Kleebe found her alone in the back room of the store.

"No Tim?" he asked.

"First day off since the beginning of the month," she said.

"Then who'll have a Christmas bump with me?" He handed her the bottle.

And he and Tess had several bumps in the back of the store and several more later that night at the Lake View Motel, but never again after that and when Walmart came to town and ran the Howells out of business, the Howells moved away.

"Somewhere like Arizona," the dull little waitress at the Town Talk Café told Kleebe. She waved vaguely to the south and the west. "Somewhere down the road."

"To all the women who moved down the road," Kleebe said, holding his glass up tipping it toward the bartender.

The bartender was playing cribbage with the local at the far end of the bar.

"You bet. All the women down the road," said the bartender, playing a card, pegging two points.

"To all the women down the road," Kleebe said to the men at the pool table.

"Fuckin' A," said the bigger pool player, hoisting his glass. "Women down the road."

"You guys in sales?" Kleebe asked.

The bigger man nodded. They kept playing pool.

"What do you sell?"

"Internet services," said the small man.

"Hair products," said the big one. "You?"

"Automotives," said Kleebe. "I'm the fucking king of automotives."

The small man pointed his cue at the Rolex dangling loosely from Kleebe's wrist. "You good?"

"I'm the king," Kleebe said. He turned to the bartender. "Set those boys up. Set your friend up. Set yourself up—and give me another."

The pool players were drinking long neck beers. The cribbage player was drinking Kessler whiskey with a beer chaser. The bartender poured Kleebe another, but passed up a free drink for himself.

"Now your prostate … It's like a blood pressure cuff wrapped around your plumbing," Arnie Slack told Kleebe years ago out by the apartment compound pool. There were single women in two-piece suits everywhere and Slack's eyes never stopped roving. "The tighter it gets, the more you got to pee. The more you got to pee, the less you can actually squirt…"

Slack was gaunt the way old smokers get gaunt—fragile gaunt, with his spine almost cupping his concave belly and chest. He repped menswear and wore plaid Sansabelts hiked nipple-high. Sitting poolside with his knees spread, he absent-mindedly displayed his once-formidable-now-useless package.

"After prostate surgery, that's all she wrote," Arnie said, his eyes darting. "You're shot all to hell. Pass me another beer."

Kleebe passed him another beer.

"I was something when I started," Arnie said. "Door-to-door. Brushes. During the war. I was big and handsome … A natural-born optimist with a Dale Carnegie smile full of teeth. The housewives couldn't say no ... For a long time there, I could sell anything to anyone in a skirt ... "

He paused, lit a Camel and burbled a rheumy cough from somewhere down deep.

"It's the arm that goes first on a ball player," he continued. "It's the reflexes on a fighter. On a salesman, it's the optimism. You reach back for a little 'can-do' and it's gone. No optimism, no new business. No new business, no momentum.

"Pretty soon, it's just you and an actuary working your turf ... Your customers start retiring and dying off ... Then, one day, phhht," said Arnie, making a fart sound with his lips. "Show's over ... Monkey died ... "

Arnie Slack took a deep drag on his Camel and paused to reflect.

"Get a load of the cans on that one," he said after awhile.

There had been three people at Slack's memorial service—four, counting the minister who had never met the man. Soderberg, who had been Slack's District Sales Manager, was there. So were Eileen, Slack's raspy-voiced, chain-smoking woman friend, and Kleebe.

"I understand he was a great salesman," the minister had said. "I hear that now that Arnie has joined his sales force, Jesus will make his sales quota this month."

They had dressed Slack in too much suit. His old alligator slip-on shoes had a new set of heels on them and the Rolex he won as Fuller Adhesive's Top Salesman, 1959, lay loose on his wrist, ticking for the time being. A pinky ring with four showy diamonds and a large garnet, shone on his spatulate, right little finger. The undertaker had dabbed make-up on the nicotine stains between his first two fingers.

After the service, when they had closed the coffin and were

wheeling Arnie off to the crematorium, Eileen handed Kleebe a brown paper bag.

"He wants you to scatter him where 15 and 23 cross in Saint Cloud," she croaked. "He said these'd compensate you for the trouble."

The Rolex and the ring were inside the bag.

"Show's over," he had said as he let Arnie's ashes fly onto the cold northwest wind. It was 3 AM in Saint Cloud and the traffic lights blinked over the empty intersection. The warning flashers on his company Ford blinked from the left turn lane, where he had parked it. Arnie Slack disappeared in a flurry, blowing south and east toward the façade of the condemned Saint Cloud Rocks baseball stadium. "Phhht. Monkey died."

"'Nother?" asked the bartender. The cribbage game was over. The local was gone.

"That should be sufficient," Kleebe said. He stood, pulled his money clip out of his pocket, peeled two twenties off and put them on the bar. "Keep the change."

"You need a lift or something?"

"A lift?" Kleebe asked.

"You're not gonna drive or anything … ?"

"Naah. Going to walk back to the Lake View and turn in. Car's back at the motel. I'm on the shoe leather express, my friend."

The bartender looked relieved.

"Good idea," he said. "They can't arrest you for walking under the influence."

Kleebe knocked the bar twice, winked and pointed a finger.

"Remember what I said. Come to terms with your balls."

"Roger that," said the bartender.

"Gentlemen—Good luck at the Silo," he said to the salesmen.

"Take it easy, Your Highness," said the small man.

"Later on down the road," said the big man as he lined up the six ball.

"Live free or die," said Kleebe.

Then he was outside in the small town summer night.

It was June and although it was nearly eleven there was still an echo of daylight in the sky and some farmer close to town had cut hay and the air was exquisitely fragrant and Kleebe walked the two blocks of Main Street, looking into the empty plate glass windows of the out-of-business storefronts on the first floors of the 100-year-old, three-story, four-square brick buildings that, like the rest of the town, had outlived their usefulness. The First State Bank, once robbed by the Barker Gang, was a video store now, with a "99-cent Tuesday" poster on the door three gran-ite steps above the sidewalk. Two hundred yards to the south, truck tires sang on the Interstate. He could see the tall yellow "Gas&Go" sign near the off ramp.

His company Ford was parked in front of his room at the Lake View and he paused to watch the gnats and bats in the aura of the last streetlight just across the narrow parking lot from where he stood.

He had always liked the way the bats swooped and homed in on the bugs, but lately he had begun to side with the gnats; to admire their insignificance and a certain fatalistic inevitability that seemed to accompany life as a speck of flying protein.

Kleebe unlocked the car and found the half pint in the glove box. Cracking the seal, he took a long pull and walked toward the light to get a better view of the carnage. Somewhere in the dark behind the motel a transformer hummed and the sound was tedious and ominous and mesmerizing. Standing beneath the light, Kleebe took another long pull, drained the bottle and left it empty at the base of the creosote-treated utility pole.

He would do it this once more for old time's sake. He would walk down the old state highway, out from under the town's feeble halo and, balls resolved for the hour and the day, put his ear to the holy concrete.

✒ *A Nearly Blonde Christmas* ✒

ALIA YUNIS

As we walked home from school, the icy snow pounded our faces like tiny nails demanding attention. I found it liberating. The more blizzards the better. Everyone had to keep piling on coats and scarves and hats until you couldn't tell if someone was fat or thin, ugly or pretty, blonde or not.

At my driveway, I raised my hand to wave good-bye to Kristin, my only and best friend at Birch Lake Elementary School, and her brother Eric. He was twelve but way bigger in his green anorak than any man I'd ever seen. As I put down my arm, the metal Wonder Woman lunch box I clutched in my hand smacked my chapped lips. They started to bleed. I licked the blood off before it froze in the sub-zero wind chill. Dusk was already setting in at 4 p.m., and I was in great pain. Not from the blood. That was pretty much a daily occurrence from November to March, ever since we'd moved to St. Paul on my fifth birthday. I was now nine and quite comfortable with cracked skin and nosebleeds.

It was the sight of our split level that made my heart ache. Eleven months of the year, our house looked exactly like every other house on the block. I basked in its suburban conformity. In this final month of the year, however, we didn't have any lights up, like the Swensons. We didn't have paper snowflakes and Frosty the Snowman pasted on the windows, like the Sorensons. We didn't have a wreath with little gold bells, like the Gundersons. We didn't even have Jesus on the lawn comfortably nestling in the arms of a woman wearing a head scarf, just like the one my grandmother, who was also from Bethlehem, wore the one time she visited us. My parents were resident aliens, and not the cute ones from outer space that my brother was obsessed with. They had American passports, but there was no doubt about it, my parents were aliens.

I wiped the remaining blood off with my snow-encrusted mitten, took an envious look at the neighbors' homes, slid down the ice on the driveway, and went inside.

My mother was in the kitchen. I could hear the TV playing the news with Walter Cronkite. I scowled as I took off my boots, hat, ear muffs, mittens, scarf, snow pants, and coat. Why couldn't she watch *The Price is Right* like everybody else's mom?

Of the gizillions of times it really stunk to be my parents' daughter, Christmas was the super stinkiest. They mistook it for a religious holiday about virgins and babies, and, since we weren't Christians, didn't think we really had to do anything about it. They were wrong.

I went into the over-heated kitchen, frowning. My mother's eyes lit up at the sight of me. I frowned harder. "If we don't put up a tree, people will think we're really weird. Isn't it bad enough that we're not blonde?" I told her, as she made yet another dinner disturbingly devoid of cream of mushroom soup.

"You know, it's not my fault your hair is curly," my mother said. "It's your father's family—have you ever seen his sisters' hair?" She sighed, knowing full well that I had never even seen a picture of his sisters, being as they were living in a country my parents still called home but could not return to. This never stopped my mother from leaping from that point to a whole list of grievances she had with my father and his gene pool. I pretended to listen, but my eyes wandered out the window as her voice went into increasingly animated waves of Arabic and English that eventually blended into familiar, vaguely annoying background static.

I looked across the white blanket separating us from Kristin's house. Mrs. Anderson, her mother, was opening a kitchen cupboard. She pulled out a bright-colored box. She looked so right in her terry cloth robe and pink curlers, with all those Christmas lights framing her in the window. I sighed. That was a mom. That was Christmas.

"That's probably Rice-a-Roni they're having at Kristin's house," I said.

My mother gave me a blank look. "You know, the San Francisco treat," I sang.

"Someday you'll grow up and get married, and you can go to San Francisco together," she said, and then she tossed excessively *fresh* vegetables into the pan. I didn't care if she had a doctorate, this woman knew nothing.

"Yummy. Something smells good." I turned to find my younger brother, Sam, a certified genius who still carried his stuffed Dick Van Dyke doll with him everywhere. He even slept with Dick. Sam was also loving and sweet and never complained, which were basically the reasons I wanted to kill him most of the time.

"They're having Rice-a-Roni at Kristin's house," I told him.

"It's okay. I like Mama's cooking, even if it doesn't come out of a box," he said. My mother smiled at him adoringly.

"Sam, we have to talk," I said. The good thing about this kid was that, even though he was smarter than me, he still respected that I was 13 months older and still a little taller. He obediently sat next to me at the dinner table.

"We have to get them organized about Christmas. We have to have Christmas," I whispered.

"Why?" he whispered back. This is when his great analytical mind started to irritate me.

"Because people think we're bizarre," I said.

"Mama says we're not," he said.

"Because *she's* bizarre," I explained. "You can't know what bizarre is if you're bizarre, dummy."

"I'm not dumb," he said. "They told me that at school."

I couldn't argue that one. "Okay, but you look dumb."

"Why?" he said. He readjusted Dick on his lap.

"Because we're the only ones that aren't decorating cookies right now. We're the only house on the whole block, maybe the whole suburb, maybe the whole state or the whole nation, that has only one color of sugar in the house," I said and leaned in closer. "Mama doesn't even realize sugar comes in green."

"What should we do?" Sam said. "Mama doesn't know how to bake. Maybe Daddy could do it."

"Sam! Dads don't bake. They fix cars," I said.

"Daddy doesn't," he said, bringing to mind the many situations in which we had witnessed this tragic flaw in our father.

"Because he's not American," I explained.

"That's not his fault."

"I know. But why should we suffer because of it?"

"I don't know. I didn't even know we were suffering."

"We are. Because we're being ridiculed by the entire block, perhaps even the entire state. Every time they make fun of your long eyelashes and my fat lips and the funny way *they* talk," I said, pointing evily at my mother. "And there's only one way to solve it."

He looked up at me all smiles. "Solve it?" he said. Now I had his attention. Sam loved to solve things. It's why he scored off the charts on math tests.

"We have to celebrate Christmas," I said. "The real way. Then we'll look normal, then people..." I saw Sam wasn't listening. My father had walked in. Short, mostly silent, and mostly bored with us, except when I was irritating him. Which usually was whenever I spoke.

"What is normal about sticking needles through popcorn so you can hang it on a tree that should be outside in nature?" my father asked. One more large problem. Besides being an immigrant, my father was a professional environmentalist long before that was "neat," cool, or even socially acceptable.

My father and I stared each other down, and I pondered whether I wanted to initiate a battle or not. I crossed my arms and decided to sit this one out, as I was somewhat hungry, hungry enough to even eat my mother's food without protesting that nothing we ate was ever advertised on television.

My mother started setting plates on the table. I looked down at the green beans and tomatoes on rice—plain, brandless rice, the kind that came in a plastic bag. I was sure that was Rice-a-Roni I saw Kristin's mother making. My life was no Christmas card.

As my parents listened to Sam reciting the wonders of his day as if there really was a Jesus and he was it, I began to put a plan into action.

Near the end of the meal, I stood up. "Santa Claus will be visiting this house even if I have to shove him down the chimney myself," I announced.

"We don't have a chimney," Sam stated.

"Well, there's just another problem this family has," I said.

"Stop it, right now," my mother jumped in. "There is no such thing as Santa Claus, and you know it. I will not have my child believing in all that capitalist propaganda. Santa Claus is not your friend. He's a fabricated sales tool for greedy merchants. Do you understand me?"

My problems mounted. Not only was my mom an immigrant, these were the salad days of her brief commitment to communism.

I was battling immigrants, environmentalists, and communists alone in the deep winter of the Minnesota heartland. And that was just at home. There were also all those blonde people out there. But I was going to have Christmas. No matter what.

"What's for dessert?" Sam said hopefully.

"Sam, dessert is for fat people living in monetary excess," my mother replied.

Sam nodded his understanding.

My mother and I forged through the crowds at Dayton's toy department. I was one of the few kids there, and my mother wasn't much bigger than me—certainly, not in comparison to the adult blondes, those broad-waisted moms I coveted. We were here because I had convinced her to take part in Phase One of my Christmas plan.

We clung to each other tightly as I tried to get her to hum along with the *Deck the Halls* muzak. Finally we approached the doll aisle. I shoved us through only to get to Giggles just as a woman was picking up the last one. My heart sank in my snowshoes. My mother, on her tiptoes, looked at me across a blonde teenager's head.

"Do we need to get you Giggles now?" she said. "We can get her for you next month," my mother moaned. "When she's on sale."

"Next month will not be Christmas. I want Giggles for

Christmas. Under the tree," I said.

"There is no tree."

"There will be. Let's go to Donaldson's. They'll have Giggles."

An excessively blonde woman looked at me sadly. "I'm sorry, honey, but I just came from there, and they're all out of her, too."

My eyes started to well up in an allergic reaction to the chocolate-mint scented candles. The woman thought I was crying.

"They'll understand that you couldn't get her for them, honey," the woman said. "Was it for your sisters?"

"No, it was for her," my mother said, as she handed me a Kleenex.

The woman looked at us strangely, slightly un-Fa-La-La-La-ish, if you ask me, and left.

"Can't we buy you another present for Christmas?" My mother was pleading but, determined to have a joyous Christmas, I could show her no mercy.

"It won't be the same," I said. "The wrapping paper I picked out for you fit perfectly with Giggles."

"Let's try and think of something else, sweetie. Oh God, will you listen to that."

My mother was listening to "The First Noel"muzak, the refrain where it says "born is the king of Israel."

"Jesus—how could he be the king of Israel?"

I shrugged. "It's just a song, Mama."

"That's how they get you. Subliminal."

During art class, we made construction paper chains for our families' Christmas trees. I liked these low key events that didn't involve having to participate with others. Miss Svenkeson approached my table.

"You're the only one who still hasn't told me what you would like to do for the Christmas pageant," Miss Svenkeson said, kneeling by my side so that I could see just how unbelievably beautiful she was with her blonde hair and blue eye shadow. I was going to look just like her when I grew up, I swore.

"Nothing, please," I begged.

"Oh, come on. Where's your Christmas spirit?"

"I really love Christmas. My whole family's just crazy about it," I said loud enough so that, hopefully, the whole class heard.

"You could tap dance," Miss Svenkeson said.

I don't really dance, and my mother doesn't know how to sew costumes," I begged harder. All true. The real reason, however, was that I was too painfully shy to perform and hide my genetic inability to be Christmasy all at the same time.

"Come on. Your brother's going to play Rudolph," Miss Svenkeson goaded.

Rudolph? I was going to kill him. He was even stereotyping himself as an outsider. He should have demanded the right to be Dancer or Prancer or any other regular member of the herd.

Kristin, quietly gluing and glittering next to me, piped in: "Maybe you could sing *The First Noel* with me?" she suggested. Kristin, until this moment, had been my one true friend because whenever they weren't making fun of my lips and Sam's eyelashes, they were making fun of her weight—or our shared incompetence with regard to flag football.

"Why, yes. That's a great idea," Miss Svenkeson beamed.

Miss Svenkeson suddenly wasn't as pretty as I used to think she was. Nor was she any longer my favorite teacher of all time. Nor could I protest her cohersion. If I did, Miss Svenkeson would call my mother, concerned about my underdeveloped interdevelopment skills, or something like that. Damn Minnesota for being so socially-conscious and progressive.

"Okay," I cried. Kristin and Miss Svenkeson smiled.

Miss Svenkeson went back to the head of class. "Boys and girls, this year for the Christmas pageant party, everyone should ask their mom to bring their family's favorite Christmas treat, so we can learn what all cultures do at Christmas—the Swedish, the Norwegians, the Danish, and even the Germans and Irish. That's why we call America a melting pot."

I looked at her excitement as she handed each kid a blue mimeograph to give our parents. She really wasn't that pretty at all.

By the time school got out, I'd forgiven Kristin. I would have been very lonely without her. We stood outside Miss Svenkeson's classroom with Sam, each holding our pile of Christmas tree paper chains.

"Listen, could you pick up Eric and take him home?" Kristin shouted through her scarf. "I got to go to Ben Franklin's and buy him and my mom and dad Christmas presents. I know you don't have to do that." I was going to tell her that wasn't true but nodded instead. My parents didn't understand allowance either, so I never carried more than milk money.

Kristin waddled off in her snowsuit. Sam and I went down the stairs to the "special people room." That's what the teachers called it. The kids mostly called it the "retard ranch," which always made Kristin fidget and blush, but she never said anything to them.

Eric, bursting out of his reindeer sweatshirt from last year, was the only one who still hadn't been picked up.

"Eric, we're going to walk home with you today. Kristin had to go somewhere," I said.

"Did something bad happen?" I forgot Eric was a worrier.

"Just Christmas," I said.

202 THE 2005 ROBERT OLEN BUTLER PRIZE STORIES

"Huh?" Eric said. "What's wrong with Christmas? It's not coming?"

"No, it's coming," I sighed. "Don't listen to me. I'm a dope." Eric smiled, reassured that I was a really big dope.

As we plunged back into the cold, someone yelled in our direction, "Booger Head." A snowball whizzed towards us and splattered and bounced off of Eric's anorak.

"Don't turn around. Keep walking," I said. Sam and Eric obeyed. I could hear Eric breathing hard.

"Which one of us do you suppose was Booger Head?" Sam asked.

"Could have been any one of us," I replied. "They didn't specify sausage lips or spider eyes or retards."

"Yep," Sam nodded.

We walked on in silence for a bit, each convinced in our heart we were Booger Head.

"Guess what...I'm going to be Rudolph in the Christmas pageant," Sam said.

I whacked his earmuff with my mitten.

"My class is going to be in the pageant too," Eric said, equally proudly, through his ski mask. "But I don't get to be Rudolph. I'm just an elf."

"You're lucky," I said.

"Oh, yeah?" Eric said.

"Yep." I said. "That's super normal." Eric smiled. He appreciated normal as much as I did.

"So what did you ask Santa for?" Eric asked Sam.

"Oh, there's no such thing as..." I stuffed my mitten in Sam's mouth.

"We asked for everything. Just like we're supposed to," I injected proudly.

Eric paused. "All I asked for was a Dick like Sam's," he worried.

"What is it with boys and Dicks?" I asked.

That night, my mother found Miss Svenkeson's mimeograph next to my homework.

"How interesting," Mama said. "I could make baklava."

Oh, God. Baklava. I knew she was going to try to make the dough herself.

Before I could protest, she came back into the room carrying a bag. She held it up.

"Look what I found," my mom smiled. She pulled a box out of the bag. Under the cellophane was Giggles.

I was still concerned about the baklava, but how could I be mad at her.

"Wow, how did you find her?" I said.

"Don't worry about that. I'm going to wrap her in the paper you gave me, and you can open her on Christmas," she said.

"We'll put her under the tree," I said.

"There is no tree," she replied by rote.

It was time for my dad and me to have that tree conversation. I sighed. One day I would discover that Valentine's Day can be more stressful than any Christmas. But that was still years away.

"Good night, Mama. Thank you for my present," I said.

"Good night, sweetie. I don't think you're supposed to thank me until Christmas."

"Mama, you have to give me about six months of allowance so I can buy you and Daddy a blender for Christmas and Sam an Easy-Bake Oven, something he would enjoy playing with me. I don't know how you'll want to wrap those."

My mother bit her lip. "Okay. Merry Christmas."

—

As the days rolled closer, as the neighbors' Christmas lights lit the snow and overpowered the morning darkness, as people's Christmas trees crowded up with presents, our house looked, sounded, and smelled agonizingly the same, despite all my efforts.

Finally, it was the second to the last day of school. The day before the Christmas pageant.

At rehearsal, Eric and his class practiced their skit on stage. The entire rest of the school was laughing at them, despite the admonishments of their teachers. I looked at Kristin, knowing her eyes would be welling up with tears.

"I wish he wasn't my brother, " Kristin said. "It's bad enough being me."

I never knew what to say to this. At least Eric wasn't always getting better grades than her. He didn't even get graded. That never seemed to comfort her.

Miss Svenkeson came up to us. "Girls, don't forget to remind your mothers to bring the treats tomorrow."

Kristin smiled. Mrs. Anderson had a real knack for mixing up different Betty Crocker cake mixes and coming up with whole new cakes no one had ever heard of before, like the orange lemon devil's food cake with peanut butter cheese frosting she made for Kristin's last birthday. Those cakes made up for Eric in Kristin's mind.

When Sam and I came home that day, we nearly tripped over a blender box and an Easy Bake Oven. To top that, the house smelled promisingly buttery, if not Christmasy. But when I took off my stocking cap, I heard my mother crying in Arabic and my father trying to comfort her. I followed her sobs into the kitchen.

She was weeping on his shoulder in front of the open oven door. Lying on the floor was a large tray of baklava flipped over and crumbled.

"I should have never tried to bake something," she wailed.

"She doesn't appreciate anything anyway," my father said. Now I knew they were talking about me.

My wish to not have baklava at school was coming true. Somehow I didn't feel happy.

"Maybe we could still rescue it," I said, making my presence known. My father glared at me. "You say that now, after she took the whole day off just to make this for you and buy us a blender we don't even want. Have you ever seen us blend anything?"

"Don't start with her," my mother said. She started to pick up the baklava in pieces, tossing them into the sink. "It's this over-indulged, materialistic society we live in. I don't want her to feel like she's not a part of it."

I started to help my mother pick up the baklava. My father stormed out. I decided then and there that I was never ever going to discuss Christmas trees with him.

"What we really make at Christmas is nothing," said Sam, bending down to help. "So I think nothing is what we should bring to the pageant." Thank God there was a genius in the house. I looked at my mother. For once, she didn't seem to be buying Sam's intelligence.

The next day, school was very hectic with preparations for the arrival of the parents. We were all backstage when they started coming. I peeked out, looking for my mother amongst the red, green, and plaid-dressed mothers. No sighting. She never liked to go anywhere empty-handed. She might not come, I thought. Oh, well, that'll be easier than having her listen to me sing that song.

The show started. Sam, of course, was brilliant as Rudolph. Kristin and I went on stage for our song. I couldn't see my mom in the audience. We started singing. I started picking up the pace, giving the song almost a *Jingle Bells* feel as I tried to get us off stage as quickly as possible. I could hear people laughing. I didn't care.

"...born is the King of Israel," we finished just as my mom walked in holding a package of Oreos. You couldn't miss her, wearing a pink dress in December.

As soon as the show was over, I fled into the audience. The Oreos, surrounded by green-sugared gingerbread men and glittery cookies shaped like candy canes, were being gobbled up. And there was my mom, surrounded by several mothers and Miss Svenkeson—all listening to her.

"Your mother was just telling me about your father's disapproval of Christmas trees," Miss Svenkeson said.

"He's a real kidder, my dad," I said.

"I'm going to talk to Principal Johanssen about it," Miss Svenkenson said. "We should have a Save the Trees Day in the spring. Hopefully, your father will be able to talk to the class." Damn my father. Damn Minnesota's liberal bend.

"I love the way you talk," one mother said to my mother.

"It's so cute," said another. My mother smiled. She looked at me.

"How come you didn't tell me you were singing a song?"

I grabbed her arm. "Please don't tell them about Santa Claus and Lenin. Please. The trees were enough."

Kristin came over with an Oreo. She handed it to me. "I got you the last one." Kristin's mother, eating an Oreo, said to my mother, "The Oreos are super. Scrumptious. We never get to eat them at Christmas, what with all the home baking I do. Is this a genuine Bethlehem tradition...well, not Oreos per say...but, well, you know, packaged goods?"

Suddenly, my mother was more popular than I could have ever hoped to be. It was horrible. I knew then that we would never be blonde, never just blend in.

"Mama, Mama," Sam said, running towards us. "They've got Eric."

Sam dragged my mother pell mell into the red and green crowd. Kristin started crying. I took her hand and started leading her forward.

A vicious group of sixth graders encircled a terrified Eric.

"We'll let you go, moron. Just as soon as you tell us how many days of Christmas there are," said the meanest one, while others laughed and mumbled undertones of "The Twelve Days of Christmas."

Eric was shaking, his face red with frustration. "I don't know. Can I go ask my sister?" Kristin was crying too hard to answer. Miss Svenkeson invaded their circle.

"All of you to the principal's office," she screamed. She was still pretty, I conceded, even when she was yelling. Kristin's mother threw her arms around Eric. He pushed her away.

"I can take care of myself," he cried. He was already much larger than her. "What kind of kids are those?" my mother complained. "What kind of question is that anyway? How many days of Christmas are there? Christmas is one day."

Maybe in Bethlehem, but not here. In Minnesota, it was one really trying, long, drawn out day. Eric looked at my mother. "You don't know how many days either?" he asked. "I don't?" she asked. "It doesn't matter anyway because Christmas is really..." She caught my anguished, pleading eyes. She stopped.

"It doesn't matter?" Eric asked.

"Actually, it isn't matter. It has no atoms. It's just a date," Sam said. The adults all gave him that "he's the second coming" look. Kristin and I looked at each other blankly. That made Eric feel better.

That Christmas, my father and I debated whether we were supposed to open the Christmas presents on Christmas Eve or Christmas day. I can't remember who won that one, but we argued it by the door that my father had decorated as if it were a tree, with tinsel and bells. My parents loved their blender from Santa, Sam and Dick loved the Easy-Bake Oven almost as much as I did, and Giggles was a joy to me for at least a couple of days. Mama even made tuna noodle casserole right from the box just for the occasion.

Eric and Kristin came over in the afternoon to show us their gifts. Eric didn't get a Dick, but he seemed to have forgotten he had asked for one. It snowed, so I guess it was a white Christmas.

I looked at Sam explaining the Easy-Bake Oven to Eric. Eric's face was painfully tense with concentration. Even if I never grew up to be blonde like Miss Svenkeson, I was not a prisoner of my own mind and body. I still could be many things. One day, I would be able to choose to stand out or to hide. I looked at Eric again. Some people can't.

I stepped outside with Giggles and stuck out my tongue to catch a few trickles of falling snow. My father was shoveling the snow on the driveway. So was every other dad on the block. Soon, Jesus would leave everyone's lawn and go into the closet with the Christmas lights. Everyone would forget there was a real Bethlehem out there. No one would care about sleigh ride songs any more, and Elton John would reclaim his place on the radio. Then my father, all covered up in his winter gear, would once again be just another guy shoveling the driveway of his unremarkable American dream. I picked up a shovel and went out to help him.

About the Winner of the 2005
Robert Olen Butler Prize

MATTHEW J. SULLIVAN received his M.F.A. from the University of Idaho and B.A. from the University of San Francisco. He has been a resident at the Yaddo Colony, and his work has been published in *The Florida Review*, *The Chattahoochee Review*, *Painted Bride Quarterly*, *580-Split*, *The Evansville Review*, *Fugue*, and *The Bloomsbury Review*. He teaches writing at Big Bend Community College in central Washington, and is currently at work on a literary mystery set in a rural zoology museum.

☙ *About the Finalists* ☙

CHERYL ALU lives in Los Angeles were she works as a screen-writer. She has written for most of the major networks and is currently writing a freelance script for a series produced by Sony Pictures Television. She began writing short stories four years ago and has studied creative writing at UCLA and in private workshop. Currently, she serves as senior editor of *Swink* literary magazine and most recently has had a story published in *The Barcelona Review*. She is at work on a collection of short stories.

JACOB M. APPEL, a graduate of the MFA program in fiction at New York University, teaches at Brown University in Providence, Rhode Island, and the Gotham Writers' Workshop in New York City. His short fiction has recently appeared in *Agni*, *Colorado Review*, *Florida Review*, *Raritan*, *Southwest Review*, *StoryQuarterly* and elsewhere. He also publishes in the field of bioethics and has written for such journals as the *Bulletin of the History of Medicine* and the *Journal of Medical Ethics*. Jacob can be found on the internet at jacobmappel.com; he welcomes email at jma38@columbia.edu.

KERRY DOLAN's stories have appeared in magazines and anthologies including *Quarterly West*, *Greensboro Review*, and *Bless*

Me, Father: Stories of Catholic Childhood (Penguin Books). She is a past winner of the Writers at Work Fiction Prize, has been a finalist for the Bakeless Prize, and she has received fellowships from the MacDowell Colony, the Millay Colony, Ucross Foundation, Virginia Center for the Creative Arts, and elsewhere. She is completing a collection of stories and a novel. A native of New York, she currently lives in San Francisco.

ALISON LEE KINNEY is a Brooklyn writer whose work has appeared in *Blue Mesa Review*, *Asian American Movement Ezine*, and *The Literary Review*, which awarded her the 2004-2005 Charles Angoff Award for her story "Term." She received an MFA in Creative Writing from The New School.

ALICIA GIFFORD is a Los Angeles area writer whose short fiction has appeared in *Narrative Magazine, Confrontation, The Barcelona Review, Ink Pot, MississippiReview.com, Best American Erotica 2005, SmokeLong Quarterly, McSweeney's Internet Tendency* and more. She won the Million Writers Award for Best Online Short Story in 2004 and she is the Fiction Editor of the literary journal *Night Train*.

PHIL LaMARCHE was a writing fellow in the Syracuse University Graduate Creative Writing Program. He was awarded the Ivan Klima Fellowship in Fiction in Prague and a Summer Literary Seminars fellowship in St. Petersburg, Russia. His story "In the Tradition of My Family," published in Volume 2 Issue 1 of *Ninth Letter*, has been made into a short film by OrLater Productions. He has recently moved back to Central New York after a year in France and now teaches creative writing at Colgate and Syracuse University. He is currently working on a revision of his first novel.

CRIS MAZZA is the author of a dozen books of fiction, including *Disability, Is It Sexual Harassment Yet?*, and the PEN Nelson Algren Award winning *How to Leave a Country*. She also has a collection of essays, *Indigenous: Growing up Californian*. A native of Southern California, Mazza grew up in San Diego County. Currently she lives 50 miles west of Chicago. She is a professor in the Program for Writers at the University of Illinois at Chicago.

JEFF PARKER'S fiction and nonfiction appear in *Ploughshares, Tin House, Columbia*, and in the anthologies *Stumbling and Raging: More Politically Inspired Fiction* (MacAdam/Cage) and *Life & Limb: Skateboarders Write from the Deep End* (Soft Skull). Jovian Books published his *The Drinking Game* this year. He teaches creative writing and hypermedia at Eastern Michigan University.

PETER PAUL SMITH is a Twin Cities-based writer.

ALIA YUNIS is a 2005 PEN Emerging Voices fellow currently completing her first novel, *The Key to the Cedar House. Alia* is the recipient of a Warner Bros. Comedy Writing award and a Women in Film comedy writing award for her one-act play, *My Date Was Late*, which she also directed at the Hudson Theatre in Hollywood. A freelance writer for many years, Alia's work has appeared in several publications, including the *Los Angeles Times* and *Saveur. Man Hunt*, an award-winning documentary she co-directed and produced, was broadcast on the Oxygen Channel in 2003. She received her B.A. from the University of Minnesota and M.A from American University.

❧ *About the 2005 Robert Olen Butler Prize* ☙

The Preliminary judges for the 2005 prize were: Megan Campbell, Matthew Dube, Jennifer Gravley, Chris Haven, and Sean Aden Lovelace. They read over 600 stories and selected these twelve to be sent on to our final judge, Robert Olen Butler, who selected "Unfound" as the winner.

Thanks to these readers and writers, and to everyone who entered.